Spur of Light

Spur of Light

Tonie Scott Ritchie

Vival Publications

2020

First published in the UK 2020 by
Vival Publications
5 Brandon Drive
Bearsden
G61 3LN
Scotland

Cover design: Vivien Martin

ISBN: 978-0-9549410-2-4

Foreword

Tonie was born in Aberdeen in 1923 and grew up in Huntly, attending Gordon School until she was 16. She worked for the Clydesdale Bank before joining the WRNS (Women's Royal Naval Service) in 1943. She travelled to Hong Kong, Malta and Gibraltar with her husband Jimmy, a Naval Surgeon, and while in Hong Kong she worked for BFBS (British Forces Broadcasting Service) as a radio announcer. They had five children – at one point she was left looking after them all plus two aged parents while her husband was away at sea.

She now lives in Plymouth, where she had formerly volunteered for the WRVS (Women's Royal Voluntary Service) and SSAFA (the Soldiers' and Sailors' Families Association), and where she returned in 1990 after Jimmy died. She then studied English at GCSE and A Level, before taking up creative writing, and having several short stories and poems published. She was a volunteer steward at Saltram House, a National Trust property, for 15 years.

This first novel was begun after Tonie attended a creative writing course on the island of Iona in 2002. It then lay unfinished for many years, until her eldest daughter encouraged her to finish it. And now, at the age of 97, she has finally completed the task.

Preface

Tonie Ritchie with daughter Pippa in 1947

When I was a child one of my favourite books was Joyce Lankester Brisley's *Milly-Molly-Mandy Stories*. Milly-Molly-Mandy, properly Millicent Margaret Amanda, had a great-aunt, and I envied her for this. Imagine my delight, therefore, when I discovered that in fact I had a great-aunt of my own! Though there, it has to be said, the similarity ended, for while Milly-Molly-Mandy's Great-Aunt Margaret was a "little, little white-haired lady in a black bonnet and dress spotted with little mauve flowers," mine was the complete opposite. Not remotely a little old lady, but rather a woman of great energy and full of fun and laughter, my Great-Aunt Tonie.

Tonie and my great-uncle seemed very exotic to us. They had travelled the world (my great-uncle was a naval surgeon) and had marvellous tales to tell. Now, very many years later, Tonie has another tale to tell and this is it. *Spur of Light*, her first novel, completed at the age of 97.

A remarkable achievement by a remarkable woman.

Vivien Martin

Acknowledgements

It was the early loss of my beloved husband Jimmy that resulted in me embarking on GCSE's, A levels and Creative writing courses in my 60's and 70's. Without our wonderful life together, and my grief after his death, I would probably not have embarked on my belated studies and writing experiences, and so this book would not have happened.

To Roselle Angwin, whose courses on creative writing in the 1990's helped me to get started with writing; and the particular course she co-organised with Kenneth C. Steven, who provided so much encouragement and stimulation, on the magical island of Iona. This course inspired me to write poems, one of which was published, won a prize, and resulted in me reading it out on Plymouth Radio.

To Eleanor Ritchie, for earlier proof reading.

To Vivien Martin (my great-niece) and her husband Allan, for their enthusiasm in 2019 which encouraged me to finish this novel. Their continued support in 2020 in final proof reading and preparation for publication has been phenomenal and much appreciated.

To my family, who have been a wonderful inspiration to me over the years, and continue to encourage me. I am so proud of them all: my children Philippa, David, Graham, Pamela and Patsy, grandchildren and great-grandchildren, and their various partners. Thank you everyone. Bless you all.

Tonie Ritchie

Plymstock, November 2020

The challenger's intelligence
is a spur of light

Seamus Heaney, *Hercules and Antaeus*

Chapter 1

1948

Years later, looking back, she could never understand why she'd had no intuition of what was going to happen that day, or the consequences it would have on her life.

The clear soprano voice of a young girl echoed round the sunny glade. The birds in the trees fringing the banks of the stream stopped their own singing, cocked their heads to one side to listen to the purity of sound. Barbara Morris loved singing in this small natural amphitheatre when she came to stay with her Great-Aunt Harriet. At sixteen, Barbara was a chubby schoolgirl with light brown hair falling over her shoulders, framing an oval face which gave a hint of prettiness when she finally fined down. Her blue eyes shone with happiness as she sang.

With a smile on her face, Barbara looked up at the birds in the trees and bowed to them before running back to the cottage, where her bag was packed, ready for when her parents came to collect her. As she entered the kitchen, she noticed that the tray was beautifully set for tea.

"They shouldn't be long now, Barbara. I could hear you practising in the glade. Your voice seems to be maturing."

"Thank you, Aunt Harriet. I somehow doubt if it will ever be good enough to sing lead parts, but I do so enjoy singing."

"Come on, girl. You've been blessed with a wonderful voice, and you must make the most of it."

Barbara's parents had gone to London for the weekend, and Aunt Harriet had picked her up from her school in West Mallet on the Friday afternoon, and taken her to her own home near Minehead. Barbara was an only child with a great love of music, and opera in particular, which her parents encouraged. In 1938, as a child of six, she had been taken to Milan's opera house, La Scala, to see Mozart's *Il Seraglio*, and had been entranced by the performance.

She remembered vividly the excitement of that evening. Her mother had insisted that she take a siesta in the afternoon so that she could stay up late. She recalled sitting in the small piazza, having a meal before the performance. She was thrilled on entering the theatre, and being conducted to one of the boxes that belonged to their Italian hosts. The boxes were lined with what Barbara thought was red damask. The chairs were covered to match and had gilt arms. The cream, gold and red of the theatre shone in the light of the enormous sparkling chandelier which hung from the centre of the vast ceiling. There was an ambience of richness about the elegant audience. The atmosphere was electric with the hum of anticipation, which calmed when the lights faded and the orchestra played the Overture. Her mother had told her the story of the opera beforehand, and the small girl had been enthralled the moment the rich red velvet curtains rose and the glorious voices of the soloists filled the theatre. The scenery and the costumes were an extravaganza of colour that she would never forget.

She had been saddened to learn that La Scala had been bombed during the war, and had been delighted when she learned that it had been rebuilt in all its former glory. It had reopened in 1946 with a gala performance.

On their return to England, she had pleaded with her parents to have her voice trained, and she now went to a Madame Charlot in the small cathedral city where they lived. Her ambition was eventually to perform in opera.

As they waited for her parents' arrival, she sat in the sunshine with her great-aunt on the bench outside the sitting-room.

"Aunt Harriet, do you miss living at Wayleigh Manor at all?" she asked.

"Yes, my dear, I do. Though not so much nowadays. I have a very busy life here, and this is my home now. I don't ever want to move from here."

"I can remember coming to stay with you there, before Uncle Peter died. It was a lovely place. Do you miss him too? He died when we were in Italy."

A sad look came over Harriet's face as she answered her great-niece. "I still miss him and always will – despite everything. 1938 was not a happy year for me. But at least I've got you and your parents nearby to keep me cheerful. You know I love having you to stay. I can remember your Uncle Peter putting you on the pony for the first time, when you were just three, and the look of fear and then wonder on your face as you realised the pleasure it gave you. Next time you come to stay we must arrange for you to go riding. There are good stables nearby."

"I'd like that very much."

Looking at her watch a frown appeared on Barbara's face. "Aren't they late? I'll just go and see if there's any sign of the car."

Harriet got up too and walked to the kitchen. She had baked some scones that morning, and the tempting aroma still lingered in the room. She checked that the strawberry jam and clotted cream were covered; just in case of flies.

Barbara came back into the house, obviously disappointed. "I suppose the roads will be busy at this time on a Sunday. I do wish they would hurry up. I'm dying to have one of your scones. They look so scrumptious."

"You always did like my scones, bless you. Want one now?"

"They're here!" cried Barbara, as she heard a car stop on the drive.

The doorbell rang and they both went to answer it. Standing on the doorstep were Sergeant Williams and a constable from the Minehead police station.

"Mrs Tremayne," said Sergeant Williams whom Harriet knew quite well.

With a feeling of dread Harriet answered. "Yes, Sergeant. What is it?"

"Please may we come in? We have some news for you, and feel it would be better if you were both sitting down."

Barbara's knees felt weak as she followed her great-aunt into the sitting room. Once they were sitting down, Sergeant Williams began, "I'm sorry to have to tell you that Mr and Mrs Morris have been involved in an accident. Someone crashed into their car on the Taunton to Willaton road."

"Oh my God!" said Harriet, glancing at Barbara, whose blanched face gazed at the Sergeant in disbelief.

"I'm afraid Mr Morris died instantly, and Mrs Morris is in a critical condition in Taunton Hospital. Can we take you to the hospital?"

There was a shocked silence in the room. Harriet shook her head as if to clear her thoughts. She rose and placed an arm round Barbara. "I think I would prefer to drive my own car there, if you don't mind. Barbara, go and get your coat. I'll get the car out of the garage."

She watched as her great-niece slowly went out of the room. Turning to the police officers she said, "Could you accompany us to the hospital, please? Then we can get there in safety and know where to park."

"Certainly Mrs Tremayne. We'll wait outside while you get ready."

Chapter 2

Harriet drove to the hospital with a set look on her face. She was in her late fifties, and had met life's hard knocks straight on. People thought of her as a hard woman, but underneath the tough exterior she was really an old softy. Her thoughts were on her niece, Annette, lying in the hospital, and also with the white-faced young girl who sat beside her in a daze. The girl hadn't spoken a word since they left the house. It was as if she was frozen.

Harriet had loved Annette as she would have loved a child of her own, if she had ever had one. Her sorrow at losing her nephew-in-law was great. He had been a very charming man, who adored his wife and child, and had left them in Harriet's care during the war, when he'd joined the Navy. John's parents had been killed in the London Blitz, and his younger brother had died in a Japanese prisoner-of-war camp after Singapore fell. So he had looked on his wife's aunt as a surrogate mother, and there was that whimsical amity between them which occurs occasionally when there is respect between two entirely opposite characters.

On arrival at the Casualty Department, a policewoman escorted them immediately to reception, where they were asked to take a seat until someone could inform them of Annette's condition. Luckily the department was experiencing a lull, and soon a young female registrar came towards them

"I believe you are Mrs Morris's aunt?" she said.

"Yes. This is her daughter Barbara. Please, can you tell us how she is?"

"I'm sorry to have to tell you that Mrs Morris is severely injured and is at present unconscious. We'll take her into surgery as soon as possible. She suffered head and face injuries, and both legs are broken. We fear there are internal

5

injuries as well. Would you like to see her before we take her to surgery?"

"Please," whispered Barbara, "Where is my father?"

"I'm afraid you can't see him at present, my dear."

Quietly the doctor said to Harriet, "Perhaps, Mrs Tremayne, it would be best if you could identify him later. We don't feel that Barbara should be subjected to that. Will you follow me please?"

Like a sleepwalker, Barbara followed her great-aunt and the doctor through double doors to an area full of medical equipment, and on into a curtained bay where her mother lay. The cuts on her face had been cleaned, but there was a large amount of bruising. Annette had been a beautiful woman, but Barbara hardly recognised her mother as she lay on the hospital bed. She gently touched her mother's left hand and lifted it to her lips.

"Mummy, please, please be all right. I need you and I love you so much."

Tears streamed down her face as she silently wept.

Harriet was talking to the registrar, who was explaining what they intended doing to try and save Annette's life. But it was evident that she was not at all optimistic.

They watched as Annette was wheeled away to the operating theatre, and with Harriet's arms round her, Barbara gave way. Her whole body shuddered with great sobs. An understanding nurse showed them into a small waiting room and said she would get some tea or coffee for them. Harriet was grateful for the hot sweet coffee; she was absolutely shattered, and for once in her life she was unsure of herself and her ability to cope. She realised that she had to, as she knew that she had been appointed Barbara's guardian. She was Barbara's only living relative if Annette died.

Four hours later, Barbara had sobbed herself to sleep in the chair, while Harriet sat silently praying to a God she did believe in, but who seemed to have deserted her in her hour of need. She'd got used to living by herself, and the thought of having to be responsible for the life of her great-niece filled her with fear. What did she know about young girls of sixteen? She thought back to her own girlhood, and realised that it was a different world for adolescents these days.

"Oh God, please give me strength," she prayed.

The door of the waiting room opened and the registrar entered accompanied, by the surgeon. George Kemp knew Harriet well. Barbara woke up with a start, and realised that something awful had occurred. Mr Kemp went over to the girl, and spoke to her, gently holding her hands. "I'm sorry, Barbara, but your mother's injuries were so extensive that we had no hope of saving her. You'll have to be a brave girl. I know your great-aunt is with you, and she will help you all she can. I am just so sorry that this accident has happened, and robbed you of both your parents."

He spoke to Harriet for some minutes, before leaving the room. He asked the registrar to attend to all the formalities, and to give some sedatives for Harriet and Barbara to take when they returned home.

Harriet straightened her shoulders and forced herself to attend to what the registrar was saying. She was bone-tired, and felt she had aged considerably during the evening. She felt that she was not fit to drive back to the village, and at any rate there would be so much she would have to attend to the next day in Taunton. She phoned friends who lived near the hospital, and they kindly offered to put them up for the night. On arrival at the Merrivales' house, they were very quickly settled in a lovely quiet bedroom.

Barbara lay in her bed listening to her great-aunt's deep breathing in the other bed. She felt it was all a horrible nightmare, and she longed for her own bed at home.

Eventually she was overcome by the sleeping draught she'd been given, and woke up the next morning to find Harriet sitting up in bed, writing on a pad of paper, with a cup of tea on the bedside table.

"Good Morning Barbara. I trust you slept well."

"Oh, Aunt Harriet. What am I going to do now?" she asked, in a soft tremulous voice.

"Come, my dear, and sit on the bed beside me. I've been thinking about that," said Harriet.

Barbara slid out of her own bed, taking her pillow with her and sat beside Harriet, who took her hand and gave it a squeeze.

"We've got a lot to do today," she said, "And I'll need your help. I know you've suffered a tremendous loss, and so have I. Your parents nominated me as your legal guardian some years ago. So any decisions made will have to be by both of us together. Until the funeral is over and we've seen the family solicitor, we cannot make any big decisions. Today we have to decide where the funeral will take place, as well as having to register the deaths. I'll do all that is necessary as far as getting in touch with the solicitor. Do you think the funeral service should be in West Mallet, or would you prefer it to be in Stickleburn? You know they had lots of friends in the Minehead area as well as in West Mallet."

Barbara sighed deeply before answering. "I think they would have liked the service to be at West Mallet. Daddy was well known there, and he and Mummy loved the Cathedral. Oh. I feel so awful. My childhood has ended so abruptly hasn't it? What am I going to do now?"

"Well to begin with, we will get up, wash and dress, and go and have some breakfast. Yes, you've got to eat something, because today is going to be a long day, and we'll have to go back to Stickleburn later to get clothes and make further arrangements. Tomorrow we'll drive to your home and make arrangements for the funeral service."

Harriet gave Barbara a hug, before getting out of bed. She disappeared to the bathroom, leaving the girl with her thoughts.

"Oh, Mummy, Daddy. What am I going to do? Dear Lord please help me." Tears welled up in her eyes, and when Harriet returned from the bathroom, she said briskly to her great-niece. "Come on, Barbara. Go and get washed and dressed, and we'll get on with things as soon as we can. It isn't going to be easy, but we've just got to carry on living. It's what your parents would wish."

Chapter 3

On returning to Stickleburn late in the afternoon of the following day, Harriet immediately set about packing a case, knowing that they would have to stay at Barbara's home for a week or so. She had arranged for an appointment with the family solicitor in West Mallet for the next afternoon. She had no idea how she was going to arrange for Barbara's future. Until she knew what the financial situation was, she was unable to make any decision.

Barbara seemed to have withdrawn into herself. It was as if she had cut herself off from the realisation that her parents were dead, and she was living in a world of her own. If her great-aunt asked her to do something, she performed it like an automaton. She only spoke in monosyllables. Harriet, who was in a state of shock herself, was fast becoming impatient with her. Barbara had the resilience of youth, while she felt antiquated. Although she was not known for her tactfulness, she forbore snapping at her niece.

She poured herself a stiff gin and tonic before the evening meal, which she hurriedly prepared. She discovered the remains of a bottle of wine in the fridge, which she drank with the cold meat and salad. There was fruit and biscuits and cheese to follow. Neither of them had much appetite, and it was with relief that once the dishes were washed and put away, Harriet sank into her comfy old chair in the sitting room, suggesting to Barbara that it might be a good idea if she went up to her room. Harriet needed time to be on her own, to come to terms with what had happened. As long as her great-niece was in sight, she couldn't afford the luxury of relaxing.

Harriet was a formidable woman, not only in stature but in attitude as well. Her late husband had been a very successful farmer, who had bred race-horses and been a keen follower of the hunt. Peter had been killed when he fell from his horse at the age of fifty-five. His death revealed that he'd been having an affair with Wendy Galbraith, the attractive widow of the man who was his head groom. The scandal had rocked Harriet off her high perch, especially when the will was read, and it was made known that Peter had left his mistress a considerable sum of money.

Harriet had decided to sell the farm, and their lovely manor house, after the estate was wound up. She had moved to the small village near Porlock. She had bought a three-bedroomed cottage with a large garden that she completely redesigned. Her interest in gardening had always been great, and she was now renowned throughout the area as an expert. She was in great demand at local shows for her talks and advice, which she gave freely and unsolicited at all times.

Ten years had passed since Peter's death, and time had eradicated any bitterness Harriet may have had. She had really loved him when they were first married. But she knew that her bossiness and her involvement with so many committees, which had taken up so much of her life then, had been the cause of the rift between them.

"No wonder you had an affair with Wendy Galbraith," she mused, "She was there for the asking, and it was obvious that she loved you too. Oh well, it was so long ago and I still love you."

She sat in the twilight with her thoughts for an hour, then painfully rose from her chair and went quietly up to Barbara's room. The door was ajar, and she could see the young girl lying in the bed. She tiptoed into the room and looked down at the sleeping girl.

"Poor love, she has cried herself to sleep," she thought.

Quietly she turned from the bed and went downstairs to lock up the cottage. She made some cocoa for herself and put some into a thermos, which she placed on her niece's bedside table, just in case Barbara woke up in the night.

As she climbed into her own bed she said to herself, "Tomorrow is another day, and I sincerely hope, God, that you make it a bit easier for us both."

Chapter 4

Two weeks later, when Harriet and Barbara returned to Stickleburn, they were both physically and mentally exhausted. The funeral had been extremely well attended, and floral tributes had overflowed the graves. John and Annette had been a very popular couple, and offers of sympathy and help from their friends were overwhelming. Once the funeral was over, Barbara appeared to be less withdrawn. Her friend, Jane Hart, had been instrumental in helping her come to terms with her loss. Although there were still occasions when Barbara was apathetic, Jane was mostly able to jolt her out of these moods.

It transpired that there were sufficient funds to allow Barbara to continue her education. Her parents had set up a trust for her, and she would inherit some of the capital when she was twenty-one. The rest was in a trust fund which she would inherit when she was thirty-five. It was decided that the house in West Mallet would be rented out to the Cathedral for the time being. It meant that, on obtaining her majority, if Barbara wished, she could either sell the house or live there.

As for continuing her education, Harriet suggested that she went as a weekly boarder to a girl's school in Taunton. Barbara was not enthusiastic about this arrangement until Jane told her that her parents were trying to coax her to attend the same school. Both girls were then keen to go. Interviews took place, and they were both accepted. They would in September embark on their studies for the Matriculation examinations, which would occupy the next two years.

During the summer holidays, Harriet decided that Barbara should have a complete break. She booked for them both to go to the south of France for three weeks, with a few days in

Paris on the return journey, so that they could indulge in a little culture. She felt they would both benefit from a change from the rationing and austerity of post-war Britain. Some friends of hers owned a house in Cannes, and had invited them to stay as long as they wished. Paul James had been a great friend of her late husband. He had married a delightful French woman before the war, and they'd lived in England until Jeanne had inherited the family home. Her only brother had fought with the Resistance during the war, and been killed while attempting to rescue two British airmen whose plane had crashed. Jeanne decided that she wished to live in a warmer climate, and so they had moved to Cannes.

One of the benefits of this became apparent once Harriet and Barbara arrived. Jeanne insisted that she took them both shopping to buy new outfits. At this time there were restrictions on the amount of money travellers were allowed to take out of Britain. Harriet agreed that they would appreciate being able to add to their wardrobe, with the proviso that she would transfer money into Paul's London bank when she returned to England. They had a wonderful shopping spree.

In Paris on their way home, Barbara's schoolgirl French was enough to allow her to get into conversation with a group of teenagers who were staying, with their parents, at the same hotel. They invited her to accompany them to the Eiffel Tower one afternoon, and she begged to be allowed to go. Harriet was finding the pace of Paris too much for her and agreed, on condition that her niece returned to the hotel in time for dinner.

Barbara set off with her five new friends. Maurice and Francine were seventeen-year-old twins, Pierre was their older cousin, and Marie and Raymonde completed the sextet. Pierre was tall, dark-haired, with a strong face and brown eyes which sparkled with fun and mischief. He was extremely good-looking, and it was obvious he intended making a play for Barbara, who over the last month or so had lost her chubbiness and now had the promise of an excellent figure. Her long hair was slightly bleached by the sun and her skin glowed with the tan she'd acquired in Cannes. She had become a very attractive young girl, with a look of innocence about her which appealed to Pierre, who, at nineteen, thought of himself as suave and sophisticated.

The view from the top of the Tower was breath-taking. All Paris lay before Barbara's eyes, and she relished the sight. She wished her parents could have enjoyed it with her. She came out of her reverie to find Pierre standing beside her. The others had started on their return to the ground.

"You were far away, Cherie," he said, putting his arm round her shoulders and drawing her close to him. Barbara was unsure of herself and tried to move away from him, although she admitted to herself that she enjoyed the closeness of his body.

Pierre kept his arm round her as they entered the lift to descend. They were the only occupants, and he drew her close again, putting both arms round her neck. Bending down, he looked into her eyes and moved his right hand to gently stroke her face, before placing his lips on hers. Barbara felt powerless in his embrace, and she enjoyed the warm feeling that flooded through her. By the time they reached ground level, she had to admit to herself that she felt excited and exhilarated by her first grown up kiss. Holding hands, they joined the others and made their way back to the hotel.

Pierre whispered that he would like to see her after dinner. Did she think she could elude her great-aunt for half an hour? They could meet on the terrace leading off the dining room at nine-thirty. Barbara was sorely tempted, and said she would try and make some excuse to her great-aunt. They usually had coffee in the lounge after dinner, and perhaps she could plead that she needed some fresh air.

Once back in her room, she flung herself on to her bed with an excited smile on her face. She debated what she should wear. She would try one of the lipsticks she'd bought in Cannes. Was this love she felt for Pierre, or was it just the satisfaction of knowing that he was attracted to her? Whatever it was, it was good for her morale, and gave her an instinctive reason to attempt to escape after dinner. The previous evening, she and Aunt Harriet had joined an English couple for coffee and Barbara had been bored stiff.

She chose a new red, black and white striped dress in the style of Dior's New Look, so popular in France. For many years during and after the war, fashion had been rather dowdy in Britain. But thanks to Jeanne, her great-aunt had bought her two new dresses at the beginning of the holiday, and she knew that the style suited her. She bathed and washed her hair, put on clean underwear and a lovely stiff white petticoat that showed off the full skirt of the dress and enhanced her small waist. She brushed her hair until it shone, and left it loose, to tumble over her shoulders. She applied the lipstick, but decided that it looked too bright, so she blotted her lips on some toilet paper until she was sure Aunt Harriet wouldn't notice. Slipping some white sandals onto her feet, she made her way to her great-aunt's room.

"Hello my dear," Harriett greeted her. "Did you enjoy yourself this afternoon?"

"Oh yes, it was wonderful," replied Barbara, and, in an effort to stop her great-aunt from enquiring too much, she proceeded to talk quickly about all she had seen.

"Obviously you've had a really splendid time with your new friends. Let's go down for dinner now."

Harriet proceeded towards the lift. As the door opened, Pierre and his parents were already occupying it. Harriet acknowledged their greetings, and Pierre's eyes met Barbara's with a questioning look. She nodded her head, blushing furiously and hoping no one had noticed. What she didn't realise was that Aunt Harriet had witnessed the episode in the mirror on the back wall of the lift.

Barbara was too tense to eat much at dinner. She longed for the meal to be over. Harriet had allowed her half a glass of wine with her meal. The trouble with that was that her face became flushed. She surreptitiously let her eyes range over the dining room, and saw Pierre sitting with his cousins and their parents. It looked as if it was a very jolly party, with lots of laughter and gaiety. She wished she could have been a member of that party, but knew that she would never have been able to understand all they were saying. Her schoolgirl French just wasn't good enough to catch all the nuances of the conversation. She decided then that she would definitely study French, knowing that it would be useful to her in the future. If possible she might be able to persuade Aunt Harriet to let her stay in France for a spell in a few years' time. Her excitement grew at the thought of her rendezvous with Pierre. She just had to escape from Aunt Harriet's beady eye after dinner.

Chapter 5

When dinner was over, Aunt Harriet moved towards the
lounge to have coffee with Mr and Mrs Roberts. Barbara
dutifully followed her, but at the door of the lounge she made
an excuse that she had a headache and wished to return to her
room. She lingered in the hall until she was sure that her
great-aunt was truly entrenched with her friends. Making her
way back to the dining room, she found that Pierre's party had
also left the room. She walked slowly over to the open
windows leading out onto the terrace. By this time the dining
room was more or less empty. She stepped out onto the
terrace, which had coloured lights strung along the hedge
leading to the garden. Tables and chairs were dotted about,
and at the far end she could see Pierre's figure leaning against
one of the trees.

As she approached him, he turned. Smiling, he held out his
hands to her. She was uncertain whether she should stay. She
was very unsure of herself, and knew that Aunt Harriet would
not have approved. But he came towards her and gave her a
gentle kiss.

"Look, there are steps leading down to the garden, and
there are seats there. Shall we go and talk?" he suggested.

"I'm not really sure whether I should," said Barbara. "I've
pleaded a headache as an excuse, so I'd better not stay too
long. No doubt, my great-aunt will come to my room to see if
I'm all right."

"Just for ten minutes, please, Cherie," pleaded Pierre,
taking her hand and leading her down the steps. They found a
seat behind a large tree, and sitting down together, he put his
left arm round her shoulders. He drew her head towards him
and kissed her. It was like nothing she had ever known. She
felt his tongue probing into her mouth, and the lovely warm

glow she had felt in the afternoon returned to her body. She felt his right hand touch her breast and she tried to move away, but he held her firmly. His hand caressed her neck, then her breast and she felt her nipple harden under his touch. Barbara knew she must stop him going any further, but she couldn't help thinking that it was a wonderful sensation. His right hand moved from her breast and she felt him raising her skirt. As his hand slipped up her thighs she came to her senses. She struggled to get free, trying to push him away. He was becoming annoyed, and in a panic Barbara managed to hit him across the face with her clenched left hand. She swiftly got to her feet.

"No, no," she cried as she ran up the steps and back into the dining room, which was luckily deserted.

Passing the lounge door, she saw Aunt Harriet was on the point of saying good night to Mr and Mrs Roberts. Dashing towards the lifts, she was fortunate that one was already there and she soon found herself outside her room. Quickly she opened the door, locking it behind her. Unzipping her dress, she hurriedly undressed and put on her pyjamas before going into the bathroom.

There was a knock on the door and the handle was tried. Another knock and she heard her great-aunt say, "Barbara are you all right?"

She flushed the lavatory and went to unlock the door, to allow her great-aunt to enter. Noticing the clothes scattered around, Harriet said, "You must have been feeling quite bad to leave your clothes like this. It is most unlike you. Get into bed. You look flushed. I wonder if you have a temperature."

Picking up Barbara's dress from the floor she gave it a shake and a few leaves fluttered to the floor. "Have you been outside, my girl? I saw that young Pierre come in as I left the lounge. He had a red mark on his cheek and he looked furious. Have you been with him? Don't lie to me please."

Barbara's eyes filled with tears as she whispered. "Yes. I sneaked out to see him on the terrace. He seemed so nice this afternoon, and I did like him. But he started to get fresh with me, and I hit him."

"Good for you. I'm glad you had the sense to hit him. He strikes me as being a little bit too cocky for my liking. I had a feeling when you made your headache an excuse, that you were up to something. Why didn't you tell me you were going to see him?"

"I felt you wouldn't have approved," answered Barbara.

"No. I probably wouldn't. But I wouldn't have stopped you if I had known where you were going to be. I'd rather you were open with me. Men and boys are always on the lookout for an easy lay."

"Aunt Harriet, how could you say such a thing?" sobbed the girl.

"Because, my dear, I'm a lot older and wiser than you, but I've not forgotten what it's like to be young and imagine oneself in love. It will happen to you often. You've grown into a very pretty young woman, but please, please, do not allow any man to take advantage of you. You'll know when you're really in love. And I would dearly like to see you happily married with a family of your own before I depart this life. Not that I have any intention of popping off for a long time. Just be careful, my dear. It's what your parents would say. Now, off to bed with you, and I'll see you in the morning. Tomorrow we'll be in London for the night, and we'll be home again the next day. Good night my dear. Sleep well."

She kissed Barbara on the forehead and turned to go. Barbara flung both arms round her great-aunt and gave her a hug. "Thank you for being so understanding. I've learned a lesson tonight that I will never forget. Goodnight Aunt Harriet. I do love you."

Once her great-aunt had left, she went over to the window, and looked out at the bright lights of Paris. She no longer felt frightened of what had happened. It had been an experience she would remember all her life, and she was determined that no-one would ever take advantage of her again. She knew that at present she was an innocent in matters of the heart, but also that she had gained some insight into what life was all about. One day, perhaps, she would fall in love and live happily ever afterwards. She had her parents' marriage to guide her. They had always been so happy in each other's company. Oh, there may have been the odd argument, but Barbara could remember that they had always come to an amicable understanding.

Thoughtfully she turned from the window and made her way to her bed. Tomorrow was another day, and soon she would be back in Stickleburn, which she now regarded as her home.

Chapter 6

Back in Stickleburn, Harriet arranged for Barbara to go riding. She was able to enjoy exploring the beautiful and lush countryside which was now her home. Jane Hart came over for a few days, and one day they decided to take a picnic along when they rode down to a deserted bay Barbara had discovered near Porlock. The sea was a brilliant blue, making a change from the usual dun-coloured water that broke on the beach at Minehead. The cliffs rose high on either side of the bay, and a small stream trickled over the sand. The girls tethered the ponies to a bush nearby, and carried the haversacks containing their food down to the beach.

They'd brought their swimming costumes with them too, and, changing into them, they hurried down to the water's edge. Jane, being much more impetuous than Barbara, splashed her way into the sea and began to swim strongly. Barbara cautiously followed, gasping at the coldness of the water. Swimming here was completely different to the swimming she'd enjoyed in the Mediterranean a few weeks earlier. Also she was slightly apprehensive about the currents, as she was not a strong swimmer.

"Jane," She shouted, "Jane, don't be silly. You're too far out, and we don't know how safe it is to swim here"

"Don't be a scaredy-cat, Babs. I'm a strong swimmer and I'm enjoying it. Come on. It's lovely".

"Young woman, come back in!" a loud male voice shouted. "There's a strong current just about where you are, and I don't want to have to come in and rescue you."

Barbara looked round in surprise at the three men standing on the beach. She had no idea who they were, and was at first frightened. But then she recognised the man who had spoken as Mr George Burgess, a farmer who was a neighbour of Aunt

Harriet's.

"Oh dear. I hope we're not trespassing," she called, "Hurry up, Jane, and swim back!"

"No, you're not trespassing Miss Morris. But we saw you ride down the valley, and hoped you weren't going swimming. The tide is on the turn,and as I said, it can be dangerous. I'm surprised your great-aunt allowed you to come here".

Barbara walked up to where her clothes were and wrapped her towel round her, shivering a little. Jane had decided that discretion was advisable, and followed her friend. She gave a flirtatious glance at the three figures standing near the water's edge. She noticed that the two younger ones were probably in their early twenties and quite good looking. One was tall and dark and the other shorter, with sandy coloured hair. Interesting, she thought.

George Burgess smiled at the girls as he said, "I don't think you've met my son Michael and his cousin Bill Franks, have you, Miss Morris?"

"Please call me Barbara. And this is my friend Jane Hart, who's staying with us at present. We go back to school next week, and were enjoying our last few days of freedom".

"Michael's due back at Agricultural College soon, and Bill is at the Medical School in Bristol. But at present they're helping with the harvest."

The two girls looked at each other, and Jane giggled before saying, "We're sorry if we worried you. We promise we won't do it again." And, turning to Barbara she added, "I think we'd better get dressed, before we both turn blue. You're almost purple with cold and your teeth are chattering."

Mr Burgess grinned at them. "We'll leave you two to get dressed. Perhaps on your way back you'd like to call in at the farm and get a cup of hot tea. You look as if you could do with it. And the boys would be delighted to have some time off. You'd be more than welcome."

Both girls thanked him, and once the men were out of sight they quickly changed into their riding habits. Jane smiled to herself as she fastened her blouse and then combed her wet hair. "Well, not an unproductive day was it Barbara?"

"You are a devil, Jane. What on earth will Aunt Harriet say? Oh! You're right. At least we've met two young men. I've not had any opportunity to meet any presentable ones yet, and these are rather dishy, aren't they? There can be no harm in having a cup of tea with them."

The two girls packed up their gear, unhitched their ponies from the nearby bush, and mounted. Riding back up the narrow country lane, they came to the gateway to the Burgess farm. They turned left, and as they rode up the drive, they noticed the well-tended sheep in the fields. As they neared the lovely old farmhouse, they saw Michael and Bill lounging against the fence of a field containing five mares and their foals. Both men turned as they saw the girls approach. Michael smiled at them as they dismounted. "At least you don't look so blue with cold. Come on into the kitchen. Mother has the kettle on. And you're lucky – it's her baking day, and she's got fresh scones and shortbread for us. We'd better hitch the ponies up first."

They followed Michael into the kitchen, where a pink-faced plump woman in her early fifties was taking a batch of biscuits out of the Aga oven, which had obviously replaced the old-fashioned range. The kitchen was warm and slightly cluttered, with a lived-in look about it which appealed to Barbara. Mrs Burgess smiled at the girls and told them to sit at the well-scrubbed table. "Bill, will you please go into the pantry and bring out some of the butter I churned yesterday?"

Barbara watched the tall young man as he did what his aunt had asked. He seemed shy and a bit reserved. She had a feeling she would like to get to know him better. Jane was busy chatting to Michael, who was not so tall as his cousin. He was stockily built, and looked as if he lived outdoors.

Michael was studying at Agricultural College at Cirencester, and Bill was in his third year at Medical School in Bristol. His father was a doctor in Devon, and Bill wanted to become a surgeon. But both young men would have to do their two years' National Service once they'd graduated.

"These scones are delicious," said Jane, "And your strawberry jam is out of this world. I wish my mother could make such scrummy jam."

"The secret is to have freshly picked fruit, and to warm the sugar before adding it to the fruit," Mrs Burgess replied.

Once they had eaten their fill of scones and shortbread, Michael suggested that he and Bill take the girls on a tour of the farm. Barbara noticed the clock on the kitchen wall, and saw that it was getting late. "Perhaps another day if you don't mind?" she said, "My great-aunt will be worried if we're too late, and we've got to return the ponies to the Gildon's stables."

"How about going to the flicks in Minehead on Saturday?" asked Michael, "When do you have to return to school?"

"Next Wednesday," answered Jane, "But I'm leaving on Sunday. Babs, do you think your great-aunt would allow us to go to Minehead on Saturday?"

"We can ask and let you know."

Saying thank you and goodbye to Mrs Burgess, the girls made their way to untie the ponies. Michael and Bill walked with them part of the way up the drive, and promised to get in touch with them about Saturday night.

On their return to Aunt Harriet's house, they found she was quite unconcerned as to the time. She had spent time in her garden, and was potting up cuttings ready for the church fete in three weeks' time. She always lost track of time when she was in her beloved garden. There she could relax and feel nothing else mattered. In fact, she was so immersed in tenderly placing the cuttings into their pots that when the girls blurted out where they'd been and who they had met, she took little notice until she had finished her work. Then she looked at them blankly. "How interesting. Did I hear you mention George Burgess?"

"Yes, Aunt Harriet. We told you we met his son and his nephew, and they would like to take us to the cinema on Saturday. Michael says he can borrow his father's car, so transport won't be a problem. Please can we go?"

"I don't see why not. They can come here first, and have something to eat before taking you out. Then I can vet them myself. I've known Michael ever since I moved here. Moira Burgess is one of the best bakers in the area. She walks off with all the prizes at the fetes. I like her. I'll phone her and arrange for the boys to come on Saturday. That suit you, girls?" She smiled happily at them before going to wash her hands in the sink in the potting shed.

Chapter 7

Within five years Barbara had graduated with honours in Modern Languages at Exeter University. She and Jane enjoyed their last two years at the school in Taunton. During the holidays their friendships with Bill and Michael grew, and they went around together to various events. Jane went on to study law in London. Both young men completed their National Service. Bill took a Short Service Commission in the Navy, while Michael served in the Army, and was now helping his father on the farm. Barbara made new friends at the University, and spent many happy hours getting to know the city and its history. While there, she took a keen interest in music, but realised that any ambition she had of becoming an opera singer was not to be.

She developed glandular fever during her second year, which had left her feeling very low. For weeks afterwards she complained of feeling a lump in her throat, and her voice was hoarse. Aunt Harriet insisted on her seeing a consultant. He discovered that two nodules had grown on her vocal cords. Arrangements were made for the removal of the nodules, and she was ordered to rest her voice for six weeks afterwards. Luckily she was on summer vacation and the weather was glorious, so she was able to recuperate in her great-aunt's garden.

Lying on a lounger one afternoon watching Aunt Harriet tending her plants, she heard footsteps and a voice she recognised said, "Hi there. I hear you've been under the weather, and I wondered if you'd like to come for a drive in the country?"

Sitting up, she saw Michael Burgess. Picking up her pad of paper and pencil she wrote. "I'd love to, but better clear it with my great-aunt."

Michael went across to Harriet, who beamed at the young man. She was very fond of him and would have been happy if Barbara and Michael fell in love with each other. But she had no intention of trying to matchmake. Michael was stockily built with broad shoulders, an angular face and brown eyes that twinkled mischievously when he smiled. His mouth and chin were strong, and his sandy hair bleached almost white by the sun. Besides helping his father on the farm, he made no secret of his ambition to convert part of the land into racing stables. He'd already had a few winners in the local point-to-point meetings. In short, he was a very likeable young man. Harriet was only too pleased for Barbara to go with him. She felt it would do her great-niece good to get out and about again.

"On your return come and have some supper with us," she said, "I've a casserole ready to put into the oven."

"Thanks, Mrs Tremayne. I'd like that."

Barbara rushed indoors to powder her nose and put on some lipstick. She ran a comb through her hair and grabbed a cardigan and a chiffon scarf, before eagerly getting into the car with Michael. She took her pad and pencil with her. There was so much she wanted to know about what was happening. She also wanted to know how Bill Franks was.

Once in the car, they made their way to Luccombe and drove up the steep road to Dunkery Hill, where they stopped to admire the view. Barbara had never been there before, and she was delighted at seeing such a panoramic view of the coastline. There was no haze over the area, and the view across the Bristol Channel was wonderfully clear. Before her spread the vista of glorious countryside, with tiny hamlets dotted here and there. It was all so peaceful. There was a lark singing high up in the clear blue sky, and the sound of other birds warbling in the bushes nearby made Barbara feel so much better. It was as if she was beginning to shrug off the awful feeling of despondency and depression she'd had since the operation. Michael told her all the local gossip, and how Bill was. He hoped to become an orthopaedic surgeon when he left the Royal Navy. He was serving on board a frigate in the Korean War.

Having caught up on all the gossip, Michael suggested they drive down to Wheddon Cross, where they had tea in a small café. They then made their way back through Dunster, where they visited the castle, which had been the home of the Luttrel family for six hundred years. Barbara was fascinated by the history, and admired the fine staircase and plasterwork. By the time they returned to Stickleburn, she realised that she would soon be completely recovered.

Back at University for her final year, she worked hard to graduate. By the time she got her degree, she had also inherited five thousand pounds from her parent's estate. She discussed with her great-aunt what to do with the house in West Mallett. She didn't want to sell it just yet, but didn't feel she could live in it by herself. It was a large double-fronted house on three floors. The Cathedral were still happy to rent it, using the basement as storage for papers, books and manuscripts.

She decided to buy herself a small car so she could be independent of Aunt Harriet for transport. Through her great-aunt, she learned that Minehead School were looking for a junior teacher of Modern Languages, and she decided to apply. She thought that perhaps a year's teaching would be good experience for her. Her ambition was still to go to France or Germany, either to teach or translate. As she got ready for her interview, she dressed carefully in a grey flannel suit and a pretty blue floral blouse. Her long hair was tied at the back with a blue ribbon. Black court shoes and handbag completed her outfit. She did not wish to appear too young, but neither did she want to look too smart.

Arriving at the school, she was shown into the Headmaster's office, where Mr Laurence, the Head of the Modern Language Department was waiting. She was told that she was not the only applicant; there were three others who'd already been interviewed. Barbara felt sure that she had no hope of obtaining the job, but spoke fluently when questions were fired at her in both French and German. She felt drained when the interview ended, and made her way into Minehead to do some shopping.

"You look like you could do with a drink."

Standing with a tall young man, Michael Burgess spoke as Barbara was passing. She'd not noticed him, as her mind was going over the interview. She stopped and smiled at Michael, then looked at the young man with dark brown hair, green deep-set eyes and a straight narrow nose. Immediately there was a frisson of attraction. He was certainly handsome and he too was smiling at her.

"Do you know Philip Sharp, Barbara? He's in charge of the securities and investment office for the Western Bank here. Philip, may I introduce you to Barbara Morris? She lives with her great-aunt, Mrs Tremayne, over at Stickleburn."

They shook hands, and Barbara felt as if an electric shock had tingled her right arm. She had never felt immediately attracted to a man before, and her thoughts were all mixed up. What with the interview and now meeting this attractive man, she felt confused.

Michael suggested they adjourn to the Quantock Arms for a drink. It was after twelve, and they could have a bite to eat as well. The others readily agreed. Philip mentioned that he'd met her great-aunt and advised her on some of her investments. Once they were sitting at a table in the pub it was as if they had known each other for ages. Philip was charming, and Barbara realised that she had never had such a rapport with anyone until now. Driving home afterwards, she relived the meeting. Would she meet him again? She sincerely hoped so. Was she falling in love with him? Did she believe in love at first sight? Time would tell.

Chapter 8

Philip Sharp was tall with dark brown hair, green eyes, a narrow nose and a square jaw. He was twenty-five years old. When he was unaware of being watched, his lips would become thin and tight, as if he were planning some strategic financial deal. His parents lived in Bristol. His two older sisters were married. Sheila had married an American during the war, and now lived in Seattle, while Mary was in Scarborough with her husband and three children. Philip was an adored only son, who had been rather spoiled by his parents. His sisters always swore that from his birth he had known how to manipulate people. His father worked in an office down by the docks, and his mother, who came from Wales, had been a nurse.

Philip shared a flat with two other men, and he was desperately trying for promotion, so that he could eventually get a place of his own. He'd made few friends in Minehead because he was cool and a bit standoffish. Michael had met him at the Cricket Club, which Philip had joined in an effort to get to know people and be seen. He'd also joined the Amateur Dramatic and Operatic Society. He'd been in the Minehead office for two years now, and had successfully studied for the banking and accountancy exams.

Outwardly he showed a charming and attentive manner towards those he wished to impress. But inwardly he was envious and sceptical of people who were wealthy: either through inherited riches, or through their own efforts. He wanted wealth for himself, but so far he'd had to be content with what he earned. He knew that he had ability and ambition, and was determined to succeed.

He'd had a few affairs with girls, but so far had not felt any strong emotions for any of them. On meeting Barbara, he found he was quite intrigued by her. She was very attractive. Slim-built, with a lithe figure that had been shown off to advantage in the grey suit she'd been wearing. Well worth cultivating her acquaintance, he thought. He knew she was well off, with the promise of more to come when her great-aunt died. On his return to the office after the meeting with Michael and Barbara, he decided to check on Mrs Tremayne's assets, and also see if he could find out the extent of Barbara's inheritance. He knew one of the solicitors who handled the great-aunt's affairs, and was quite sure that with a little subtle probing, he could somehow get information on what Barbara's inheritance was worth. If, as he suspected, she was rich, then he decided he would definitely attempt to charm her. She was just the type of wife who could help him in his career.

Philip Sharp was a determined and selfish man, and greedy for the good things in life. But he hid it under a charming manner that had fooled a lot of people.

A few days later, Barbara was feeling particularly pleased with herself. She'd heard that morning that she'd been appointed to the position of teacher of Modern Languages at the school in Minehead. She was delighted not only for herself, but also for her great-aunt. It meant that she could continue to live with her and keep an eye on her.

The previous winter Harriet had suffered a particularly virulent bout of flu, which had left her feeling tired and listless. Her spirit was undiminished, and she still enjoyed her gardening and the talks she undertook. But she tired easily, and it was obvious to Barbara that her great-aunt was beginning to feel her age. She felt very protective towards her, and realised how much she owed to Aunt Harriet. She still missed her parents very much, but knew how lucky she'd been in having her great-aunt as her guardian. She loved

Harriet dearly. The old-fashioned ideas of morality had been instilled into Barbara, and she would never do anything to hurt Harriet. She'd had flirtations at University, but knew where to draw the line. Boyfriends were inclined to think of her as cool and slightly frigid. Little did they know how passionate she could feel. The episode in Paris with Pierre had taught her a lot, and despite all the teasing of her friends at Exeter, she was determined to remain a virgin until or if she married.

She was thinking of the meeting with Michael a few days ago and of Philip Sharp. He had not been far from her thoughts ever since, and she sincerely hoped she would see him again. The phone rang early one evening, and she ran to answer it. Meanwhile, Aunt Harriet was sitting in the garden enjoying the evening sun with a gin and tonic in her hand.

"Five four seven nine," said Barbara, having picked up the receiver.

"Is that Miss Morris?"

"Yes," she answered, recognising the voice.

"It's Philip Sharp here. We met a few days ago with Michael Burgess."

"Yes, I remember. How are you?"

"I'm well and wondering if you'd care to have dinner with me one evening next week. The local Amateur Operatic Society are putting on *Iolanthe* at the theatre, and I could get tickets if you'd like. I'm a member, but I'm not taking an active part in this production."

"Why Philip, I'd love to. And I have something to celebrate. I've got the position at the school, and I start in September. My great-aunt is delighted and so am I."

"That's great news. Congratulations. This means I might be able to see more of you. Which day next week would suit you?"

"I'm playing in a tennis match on Tuesday evening, but

apart from that I'm free, as far as I know."

"Right. I'll get back to you when I've got the tickets. I'm looking forward to seeing you again."

"Thank you." She replaced the receiver and gave a little cry of "Yippee," before hurrying out to join Aunt Harriet, and tell her about the phone call and the invitation

When she returned to the garden, Aunt Harriet was out of the chair and dead-heading some roses.

"That was Philip Sharp on the phone, asking me to go to the theatre with him next week and to have dinner with him. He's going to ring me when he gets the tickets."

"Philip Sharp?" queried Harriet. "Oh, you mean the young man from the bank whom you met with Michael the other day?"

From the tone of her great-aunt's voice, Barbara got the impression that she wasn't over-enthusiastic about Philip Sharp.

"Sharp by name and sharp by nature," she thought she heard Harriet say to herself.

Chapter 9

Standing in her bedroom, looking out of the window, Barbara watched her great-aunt strolling round the garden. Harriet, as usual, had her gardening gloves on, with secateurs in her hand and the old basket on her other arm. This was her evening ritual. During the day Harriet would be busy weeding, planting and nourishing her beloved flowers. But after a cup of tea and a sit-down about four, she set about dead-heading her roses, which grew in abundance. The scent of them could sometimes be overpowering, and the fragrance reached Barbara's room. She sensed that Harriet was not really very keen on her going out to dinner and the theatre with Philip Sharp, but she didn't have the nerve to question her great-aunt about her feelings. It was not that Harriet had disapproved or said anything about Philip. There was just a niggling feeling that her shrewd great-aunt was not enamoured of him.

She shrugged her shoulders. She was twenty-one years old, and quite capable of making her own decisions about her friends. She liked what she had seen of Philip. He had been charming and attentive when they met. There was no reason at all for her to doubt her own feelings. She was going to enjoy tonight, and didn't care what her great-aunt thought.

She had bathed and washed her hair, which hung on her shoulders in a pageboy bob. The creamy skin of her face was lightly dusted with powder, and her eyebrows brushed with a touch of mascara. She applied pale pink lipstick to her lips. Standing back from the mirror, she thought to herself that she looked quite presentable. She decided on a cream linen dress with pale pink edging at the neckline and sleeves. Opening the door of the old walnut wardrobe, she picked a pink cardigan from the shelf. It exactly matched the pale pink on the dress. Barbara congratulated herself on being fortunate in buying the cardigan when she had bought the dress. It made a smart outfit. At least, she thought it did.

She went out into the garden to say goodbye to her great-aunt, before getting into her little blue car. It was an MG sports car. She would really have preferred a red one, but she remembered someone at Exeter telling her that the police picked on people who drove red sports cars. Driving out of the gate, she waved a hand to Aunt Harriet, and turning left, drove towards Minehead, with the sun behind her. She loved the feel of the wind in her hair and the freedom of having her own transport. Philip had offered to come and pick her up, but she'd said that she would prefer to drive herself. She parked the car near the Queen's Hotel on the seafront. The tide was in, lapping the walls on the Promenade. Boats were bobbing in the harbour, with seagulls crying raucously above. In the Channel there were a few yachts, their sails white against the blue of the sea.

Philip touched her arm as she locked the car. "I saw you drive in," he said, "It's lovely to see you again. We should have plenty of time to enjoy our meal before the theatre. That's why I suggested we meet early. I hope you didn't mind?"

"Not at all, Philip. We don't want to suffer from indigestion during *Iolanthe*, do we?" She smiled up at him.

They crossed the road to the hotel, and entered the restaurant, where they were shown to a table overlooking the bay. There were two other couples sitting at a table nearby. Once seated, the waiter handed them the menu.

"Would you care for a sherry, Barbara?" Philip asked.

"Yes please. Dry for me."

"Two dry sherries please, and we'll decide on the menu while you fetch them."

The meal was delicious. Barbara had paté to start with, followed by Sole Veronique and a fruit flan for dessert. Philip chose soup, then steak and mushrooms, with the fruit flan to follow. They had a carafe of rosé house wine to accompany the meal. Neither of them wished to have coffee. At 7.45 they were ready for the short walk to the theatre.

"That was delicious Philip. I've never had a meal there. Usually when we go out for a meal, it's to Porlock where my great-aunt knows the owners of the Ship Inn. I must tell her how delicious the food is at the Queen's."

"I'm glad you enjoyed it. We must do it again."

Philip tucked Barbara's arm under his, and they walked and talked companionably along to the theatre. The production was a typically amateur one, with a few minor hiccups. The high notes of the soprano who took the part of Iolanthe were rather forced. At least Barbara thought so, but didn't like to criticise her to Philip. After the performance they wandered back to where Barbara had parked her car. She offered Philip a lift to his flat, but he reluctantly refused, saying, "It's not very far, and the walk will do me good. By the way, I've wondered why don't you join the Operatic Society? You're interested in music, and I gathered from Michael that you've an excellent voice. It would also give us more opportunity to meet."

"Well, if I'm staying in this area for some time, I suppose I should have some more interests. I'll discuss it with my great-aunt and see what she says. She's very knowledgeable about this whole area. Yes, I'll definitely consider it. Now I must get back, before she starts worrying. Bless her, she clucks around me like a mother hen. Oh, I really shouldn't say that should I? She's been truly marvellous to me ever since my parents died, and I'd hate to hurt her. Thanks, Philip, for a lovely evening. I've really enjoyed myself."

"So did I," said Philip, leaning on the car door before he closed it. He bent forward and gently kissed Barbara on her lips, placing his arm across her shoulders. As he drew away, he looked into her eyes, and once again bent to kiss her, knowing that she wanted him to. This time Barbara responded, and her lips opened to receive his kiss.

Philip knew he had aroused her sensual feelings, but he also knew when not to overstep the mark. "Goodnight, my dear," he said, "I've really enjoyed myself tonight. I'll be in touch with you very soon."

He removed his hand from the car door and watched as she started the engine. She waved a hand to him, and set off. Her feelings and emotions were in turmoil. She had wanted more kisses. In fact she realised that she wanted him.

Philip walked back to his flat, assured that he'd behaved with restraint and good manners. Having had dealings with Mrs Tremayne, he knew he'd have to tread carefully in pursuit of her great-niece. But he also knew that he had whetted Barbara's appetite for his attention, and was quite sure that she would succumb to his charm eventually. He decided that he would proceed with care, and take his time. He felt that in doing so, Barbara would become extremely keen. She was young and inexperienced, and he gained pleasure in the knowledge that if he was successful and did marry her, not only would he gain a wealthy wife, but one he could initiate into enjoying his lovemaking. Yes, life was looking up.

During the next few weeks, Barbara and Philip enjoyed each other's company tremendously. Barbara's pleasure in the relationship deepened. Even Harriet had to admit that her great-niece seemed to glow with happiness, and although she had her reservations about Philip, it was obvious to her that Barbara was in love.

"Why don't you ask Philip to come to lunch with us next Sunday?" she suggested one day.

"I rather think he's supposed to be going to see his parents in Bristol. But I'll ask him anyway. You'll like him, Aunt Harriet, once you get to know him."

There goes innocence, thought Harriet. She began to wonder if perhaps she'd been too old-fashioned in her ideas of coping with Barbara after her parents had died. Life had changed so much since she was young, and these days it seemed that the world was galloping to disaster. No sooner was the war over in 1945, than the world was hurtled into another dispute in Korea. She'd heard from Moira Burgess that her nephew Bill Franks was serving as a Medical Officer on board a frigate operating off the coasts of Korea. His mother was extremely worried about him, but Bill seemed to be enjoying it. They had spells in Sasebo in Japan, and were often down in Hong Kong for refits. He was certainly seeing a lot of the world, and was wondering if he should apply for a permanent commission. But he was still keen on becoming an orthopaedic surgeon. It seemed he was getting some practice at the Naval Hospital in Hong Kong when the frigate was in port.

Harriet wished Barbara had met him again before he went off to Korea. They'd got on so well together. Oh well, what will be will be, mused Harriet, as she hoed the weeds in the border.

Barbara was due to start teaching the next week, and was slightly apprehensive about how she would perform. She hoped she'd be able to control her pupils. Although she'd had some teaching practice in her final year at University, she was still anxious about teaching senior pupils. The senior pupils could be the most rewarding to teach. Barbara was a gentle person, but she had a strong sense of discipline, and hoped that she could cope.

She applied to join the Operatic Society, and attended an audition, which she easily passed. Soon it would be time for the decision on what the next production would be, and she was looking forward eagerly to the start of rehearsals. It meant she would stay in Minehead after school; probably have a bite to eat with Philip, she hoped, before going on to the hall. Although Philip said he loved music, he was not a singer. But he could play the piano and violin, so he would be in demand as a musician. Barbara was confident that Philip was the love of her life, and that he would eventually propose. She spent ages daydreaming about what their life together would be like.

Philip had been careful of his behaviour with her. His kisses were warm and tender, and his caresses had stayed above the waist. A gentle touch on her breast was enough to make her knees go weak and a delicious warm feeling to flow inside her. She wished for more, much more, but it was as if he was biding his time before attempting to take further liberties with her.

In fact, he was being clever and cunning in his method of wooing her. He wished to be accepted by Mrs Tremayne before he made his move, and when Barbara issued the invitation to lunch on the following Sunday, he was elated. "I'd love to accept the invitation," he replied, "I'll phone my parents and say I'll be up the following weekend. Thank your great-aunt for me will you please? What time do you want me to arrive?"

"Twelve thirty for one o'clock. Aunt Harriet has asked the Burgesses, and Sir Robert and Lady McAllan from Porlock, so there will be eight of us."

"Damn" thought Philip disappointedly. He would much prefer to have had a quiet meal, just the three of them. His prospects of impressing Mrs Tremayne would have been greater, he felt. Little did he know that Harriet wished to see how he would react in a social atmosphere. She knew he'd won a scholarship to a grammar school, and that since then he'd done well. Yes, she knew she was a snob, but she reluctantly admired him in obtaining success in his career. However, she still had her reservations about him, and was interested to see how he would comport himself on Sunday.

Chapter 10

Sunday dawned bright and sunny, and promptly at 12.30 Philip arrived at the door, to be greeted by a smiling Barbara. "I'm glad you've arrived on time. You can help me with the drinks. We'll have them outside. Oh, are those for me?" Barbara asked, as she noticed a parcel in his hand.

"No they are not for you, you greedy girl! They're for your great-aunt. Ah, hello, Mrs Tremayne. Thank you so much for inviting me. What a charming house you have." He held out the box of chocolates to Harriet, who smiled as she received them.

"Come through to the garden Philip. As it's such a lovely day, I felt we'd better take advantage of the sun. Barbara will you bring the others out when they arrive?"

She turned and led the way through the sitting room and out on to the terrace, which ran the length of the back of the house. Philip would have preferred to linger in the sitting room. He'd noticed some really lovely furniture and paintings, which he was quite sure were antiques. Sitting herself on a bench, Harriet motioned Philip to come and sit beside her. Barbara brought out a silver tray on which were three glasses of sherry. She handed one to her great-aunt and another to Philip, before placing her own glass on a wrought iron table. Then the doorbell rang, and she went to answer the door.

Harriet turned to Philip and said quietly, "You and Barbara have become very friendly in the last few weeks haven't you?"

"Yes, Mrs Tremayne. I have become very fond of Barbara. We get on so well together, and I'm so pleased she got the job at the school. I hope we continue to see lots of each other. That is, if you don't object."

"Barbara is over twenty-one. All I want is her happiness. I'd hate to see her hurt by you or anyone." There was a cool warning note in Harriet's voice as she spoke.

"Oh, hello Doreen and Robert," she called, as she noticed the guests arrive. "Is Barbara fixing you drinks? Come and meet her friend Philip Sharp. Philip this is Sir Robert and Lady McAllan, who own Priory House near Porlock."

Philip stood up as the guests came out on to the terrace, and shook hands with them. Sir Robert was a large man with a tanned leathery face and a drooping moustache. He'd been in the Diplomatic Service, and had spent most of his life in the Middle East until his retirement. Doreen, his wife, was petite with dyed blonde hair and a rather sulky expression on her face. Both were in their sixties.

"My dear Harriet," said Lady McAllan in a rather shrill, high-pitched voice, "Your garden is always so exquisite. How hard you work at it. No wonder your hands are so rough. I don't know how you cope with it all. I hate gardening. Do you like gardening Mr Sharp?"

"Well, Lady McAllan, I've not really had much to do with gardens so far. I was brought up in Bristol, and we didn't have much of a garden there. Since leaving school I've not had time to take an interest. But one day I hope I shall."

"Oh, and what do you do?"

"I'm in the Security and Investment Department of the Western Bank in Minehead."

"Really. Robert, did you hear that? We have a financial wizard here."

At that point Barbara ushered George and Margaret Burgess out into the garden, and Philip breathed a sigh of relief. Michael followed Barbara, carrying a tray of drinks for the newcomers. Having served the McAllans their gin and tonic, and his parents their sherry, he grabbed his own tankard of beer and approached Philip.

"Thank God you arrived when you did." Philip said quietly. "I was being interrogated by Lady McAllan, and although she's so small, she seems quite a formidable lady."

"She's not so bad once you get to know her. It's her voice that grates a bit." Michael grinned at Barbara, who'd joined them. "Well my girl, how are you liking the work at the school. Or is it too early to say? Some of those children are rowdy. The best of luck to you. You'll need it at that school. I should know. I was a pupil there myself."

Barbara punched his arm playfully. "Thank you very much. You're trying to take my confidence away from me before I've had a chance to show how good I am. I hate you."

"Luncheon should be ready," said Harriet. "Shall we go in? Barbara you know the seating plan. Then you can help me with the tray."

"Let me help," offered Philip. "I've a strong pair of hands."

Harriet was a little surprised by his offer, but gratefully accepted it. Philip had offered because he wished to see more of the house, as well as ingratiating himself with his hostess. He was impressed by the dining room, with its lovely old mahogany table, chairs and sideboard. He was told to place the tray on a beautiful side table, which he recognised as Hepplewhite. The walls were covered with a light green and gold striped paper that matched the chair seats, At the window, golden-coloured velvet curtains were draped in heavy folds. The paintings on the wall were of hunting scenes, and Philip noticed that the one above the fireplace was definitely by Stubbs.

Lunch was delicious and the conversation flowed. Philip sat on Harriet's left, with Sir Robert on her right. Next to Philip was Lady McAllan, who divided her attention between Philip and George Burgess. Harriet smiled inwardly to herself, as she knew Philip was finding Doreen heavy going, but was struggling valiantly with her, as well as talking about financial and political affairs with Sir Robert and herself. He was acquitting himself extremely well, and Harriet was impressed, despite her previous misgivings.

Coffee was served on the terrace, and at about three o'clock the others made their departures. Barbara told Philip to stay while farewells were said.

"That was a good party, Aunt Harriet. Now, I suggest you go for a rest, and Philip and I will tidy up and do the dishes."

"All right my dear," said her great-aunt. I must admit I could do with putting my feet up for an hour. Thank you Philip. I'll see you later. Tea will be about four thirty."

Barbara looked across at Philip, who was stacking plates on the kitchen table prior to their being put away. They had cleared the dining room of all the debris of lunch. Barbara had washed the dishes while Philip dried. It was not something Philip was used to doing. His older sisters had been the ones in the family who helped with the domestic chores, but living in digs with two men, he had taken his share in attempting to keep the flat clean and tidy. Now it had stood him in good stead.

"There, it's all finished." said Barbara, as she mopped up the water on the draining board. "I'll just put the dishes away, and then we too can sit down. Aunt Harriet will be in her favourite chair in the sitting room, with her feet on the old piano stool."

As she completed placing the pans in their respective shelves, she felt Philip's arms come round her waist and as she straightened up he kissed the nape of her neck and nibbled her ear. She turned in his arms and put her hands behind his neck. They looked at each other, and slowly he lowered his head to kiss her lips. They clung together until they had to come up for air. Breathlessly Barbara said, "Let's creep out the back door and go into the garden."

Once on the terrace, Philip grabbed two cushions from the bench, tucked them under his arm and, taking hold of Barbara's hand, he led her down onto the grass far away from the house, and out of sight and sound of Harriet. Placing the cushions on the grass behind a clump of buddleia bushes, they sat down. The sun was hot, and there was the hum of bees and the flutter of butterflies wings as Philip pulled Barbara into his arms again.

"Darling Barbara. I've been longing to say this to you for ages, but felt that we had known each other for such a short time. I love you so much. Will you marry me?"

With no hesitation whatsoever Barbara replied. "Yes Philip my love. I've loved you since we first met. Oh, I'm so happy. I do love you very much. Do let's tell Aunt Harriet."

Philip's face fell, and Barbara was puzzled until he spoke. "I don't think we should announce it just yet. Let's give your great-aunt more time to get to know me. It can be our secret, and we could possibly announce it at Christmas. What do you think?"

On consideration Barbara had to agree with him. He explained that there were promotions to be announced shortly at the bank, and that he was waiting for the results of his accountancy exams. If successful, it would definitely mean promotion, and possibly a move from Minehead to a bigger branch. Barbara was upset at that thought, but cheered up when Philip suggested getting married next summer. This would give him more time to save up towards buying a house, and also give Barbara a year teaching at the school.

"But Philip, I have a house in West Mallet which I can sell, and we can buy one where you work. As for furniture, there's an attic in the house full of my parents' furniture. There are some lovely things that belonged to my grandparents, so we will not have to buy much."

This was exactly what Philip had envisaged and hoped she would say. However, he protested. "That's yours darling. I'm old-fashioned enough to wish to provide for my wife myself. But we can discuss it later. I love you and you have promised to marry me. That is enough for me at present."

Then, glancing at his watch he added, "It's time for tea. Let's go and make it before your great-aunt wakes up. And then I should go. I mustn't overstay my welcome on my first visit, must I? I do want to do the right thing, so that she likes me and trusts me."

Chapter 11

By the following December Barbara found she had enjoyed her first term at the school. Mr Laurence was pleased with her teaching ability. The pupils were obviously enjoying the French and German lessons with her, as their end of term exam results showed great improvement.

On Thursday evenings she stayed at school, marking her pupil's work and preparing lessons for the next week. Then she met Philip for something to eat, before attending rehearsals for the next production of the Operatic and Dramatic Society. The meetings were held in a draughty, drab hall belonging to the local church. It had been decided to put on a pantomime before Christmas. Barbara had been chosen to play the part of Alice Fitzwarren in *Dick Whittington*. Julie Brown, who had sung the part of Iolanthe in the summer production, was to play Dick. She was envious of Barbara's singing ability. What Barbara didn't realise was that Julie and Philip had had a short affair previously, and Julie had never really got over her feelings for Philip. As the date for the performances drew near, Julie did her best to upset Barbara. On one recent occasion she had reduced Barbara almost to tears. After the rehearsal, instead of going for a drink with most of the cast, Philip suggested that he take Barbara back to his flat where they could sit quietly until she had composed herself before returning to Stickleburn.

Once in the flat, Philip made coffee and they sat in the kitchen together, talking over what they intended doing after Christmas. Philip had passed his accountancy exams, and was being appointed to a bigger branch of the bank at Taunton in the New Year. He wanted to announce their engagement during Christmas, and asked Barbara to come with him on Saturday to choose a ring. While they were discussing their future plans, David and Bob, his flatmates arrived home. Philip was rather annoyed by their intrusion, and suggested that they leave the kitchen for the privacy of his bedroom. This brought a few coarse comments from David and Bob. Barbara gave them a frosty look which made them apologetic.

"We never seem to get much chance to be alone these days do we?" she said to Philip. "We're both so busy, and even at the weekends we're usually either with my great-aunt or you're in Bristol with your parents. I'm getting fed up with it all. Aunt Harriet has accepted you, and I'm sure it'll be no surprise to her if we do tell her we're engaged."

Barbara was sitting on the one chair in the bedroom, while Philip perched on the edge of the single bed.

"Come over here darling and sit beside me," he replied. "Tell me what kind of ring you'd like. I can't afford the Koh-i-Noor just yet, but one of these days you'll have expensive jewellery, I promise you."

"I don't want jewellery my love. All I want is you."

Barbara put her arms round Philip's neck and kissed him with passion. He was rather taken aback by Barbara taking the initiative, and returned her kiss eagerly. They fell back on the bed and his hands started to unbutton her blouse. She showed no sign of resistance, and he gently lifted her so he could undo her bra. He then nuzzled her breasts until her nipples hardened and stood erect. She moaned softly as his hands slipped down to her thighs. He lifted her skirt and his hand slipped under her pants. She felt moist to his touch – ripe for the picking, he thought, as his own desire surged up. He let his finger enter her and gently stroke her. Her hips moved in time to his stroking, and suddenly she cried out as an explosion of pleasurable warmth flooded her body. Philip knew that he had brought her to orgasm, and also realised that his own desire was great. He had enough sense however, to know that he must not take advantage of her. Later, perhaps when they were formally engaged.

"Darling, I think you had better go, before I really forget myself. I love you too much to go too far with you just now."

Her flushed face on the pillow, and the soft expression in her eyes, told him that she was his for the asking, but sense prevailed. He pulled down her skirt and sat up on the bed. Slowly she fastened her bra and buttoned her blouse with fingers that shook. She had just experienced the most wonderful sensual feeling that had left her aching for more.

"Philip let's tell Aunt Harriet this weekend. Then we can make plans for the wedding. I want the world to know that I'm yours."

"Alright darling. We'll tell her on Saturday, and see what she says. I only hope she approves. Not that it really matters, as nothing is going to stop us getting married, now that I've got promotion. Come on, you'd better get back before your great-aunt sends out a search party. It's late and you know she worries until you're home."

As she drove home, Barbara hummed happily to herself. She parked the car in the garage and walked round to the front door, noticing that Aunt Harriet's light was still on. As she let herself into the house, she swore under her breath and thought she'd better comb her hair before she went upstairs. She decided to make herself a cup of cocoa to give herself more time before facing her great-aunt. She wandered into the warm kitchen. The ginger cat opened his eyes as he lay in his basket by the Aga, yawned and stretched his paws before closing his eyes again. He wasn't going to be disturbed as Barbara waited for the milk to boil.

"Did the rehearsal go on longer tonight?" called Harriet as Barbara came upstairs.

"Sorry, but there was a bit of trouble tonight between Julie and myself. She succeeded in upsetting me, and Philip took me back to his flat so I could recover. Julie is becoming a pain, and I sometimes wish I'd never joined the Operatic Society. I'm afraid we forgot the time. I'm sorry for keeping you awake, but you know you shouldn't worry about me."

"Bless you, dear. I do worry because I'm fond of you. I only hope Philip takes care of you."

Barbara felt her face flush as she bent to kiss her great-aunt goodnight.

"He takes great care of me. I love him and he loves me. He's coming over on Saturday. We're going into Taunton first, and we'll be back for supper. Is that all right with you?"

"Yes, I suppose so," answered Harriet. "Close the door will you dear? Goodnight. See you in the morning."

With relief, Barbara closed the door and made her way to her own bedroom.

Chapter 12

On the Saturday, Barbara and Philip drove to Taunton to buy the engagement ring. They chose one with two diamonds on either side of a sapphire. Barbara was thrilled with it. They then returned to Stickleburn for tea. While Barbara was in the kitchen setting the tray and waiting for the kettle to boil, Philip went into the sitting room to talk to Harriet. Now was the time to approach her about the engagement.

"Mrs Tremayne, I've something I want to ask you, and I hope you will give me an honest answer."

"Well Philip, I'll try to the best of my ability."

"I love Barbara and she loves me. As you know I've got promotion, and have passed my accountancy exams. I move to Taunton in the New Year. I've asked Barbara to marry me, and she has said yes. But I would like your approval."

"I could see this was coming for quite a while," said Harriet with a wry smile. "I doubt if I could prevent it happening, could I? I personally think Barbara should have a few more years teaching before she thinks of marrying. But I don't think she will be prepared to wait. When were you thinking of getting married?"

"Sometime in the summer, But we'll have to spend some time beforehand looking for a house to buy. I've got enough saved up for a deposit, and the bank will let us have a mortgage at a low interest rate."

"We'll have to have a discussion about that. As you know Barbara owns a house in West Mallet. We'll have to go to see our solicitor, Mr McGrath."

At that moment the sitting room door opened and Barbara entered, carrying the tray, which she placed on the table beside her great-aunt's chair. Harriet didn't notice the black look that came over Philip's face as he realised that the solicitor was going to be consulted.

"Congratulations are in order I gather," she said to Barbara, "Are you happy? Come and give me a kiss."

"Oh yes, Aunt Harriet. I'm so glad you approve. Look at my lovely ring."

She held out her left hand and Harriet duly admired the ring.

"Well," she said, "We'll have to start organising things for the summer then. I presume you'll want to be married in Luccombe Church. Oh, before you pour the tea, please go and put a bottle of champagne in the fridge. We'll have to celebrate this evening. There is a case of Moet et Chandon in the pantry, under the bottom shelf."

Barbara did as she was told. Before she returned Harriet looked at Philip and said sternly, "You'd better make her happy, or you'll have to answer to me."

"I have every intention of making her happy. I know how lucky I am that she has accepted my proposal."

After tea, the two young people went for a short walk. The light was fading as they walked along the lane. The hedgerows were bare, and in the sky the starlings were swooping in a black cloud before descending to roost overnight on the ruined barn at the end of the lane. There was a frosty nip in the air as well as the smell of wood smoke as the couple turned to make their way back to the cottage.

The aroma of roasting chicken assailed their nostrils as they came through the door. Harriet had decided to get on with cooking the dinner while they'd been absent. Barbara had prepared all the vegetables in the morning, as well as making an apple pie. Under her great-aunt's guidance, she was becoming quite proficient at cooking. Hanging up their coats in the hall cupboard, Barbara whispered to Philip, "You go and read the papers while I go and help Aunt Harriet. I think she'd probably like a few words with me on our own before we open the champagne. I'll set the table too."

She kissed him hurriedly and made her way into the kitchen.

"Oh, you're back already," said Harriet. "You look like the cat that's been at the cream. It's obvious you love him. I just hope he's worthy of you. But then I'm prejudiced, as I'm sure your parents would have been. Just be happy my dear, and make sure you keep a tight rein on him. Look what happened to me. I put my own interests before Peter's. No wonder he wandered. But I'm sure you'll be more sensible. Can you set the table, dear? Then we'll open the champagne. We'll have to see Mr McGrath in the New Year, and arrange for the house in West Mallet to be sold so that you can buy something in Taunton. That is, unless you want to keep it."

"No I don't. I feel we should look for something similar in Taunton, so that we have plenty of room for when we have a family."

"Heavens above, child! Let's get you married before you start thinking about children. And no jumping the gun girl."

Barbara felt her face going red as she smiled at her great-aunt. "No. I've no intention of that. I'd hate to get married with a bump showing. I'd not be able to get into Mummy's dress, and I want to wear it if it's possible. We'll have to sort out the furniture and stuff in the house, won't we?"

"Yes. But I've got your Mother's dress and the veil all folded up in tissue paper in a box in my room. I didn't want to leave it in the house with all the other things. Your Mother's jewellery is with Mr McGrath, and you should have got it on your twenty first birthday. Never mind, it'll still be there. Now, set the table, and then we'll celebrate."

There was a festive atmosphere in the house that evening. Various ideas were suggested for the wedding reception, and it was agreed that it should be held in the garden at Stickleburn, with a large marquee and caterers hired. Harriet was delighted to be able to use her expertise in advising the young couple.

At one point Philip felt he was taking a back seat, and began to resent that his nose was being put out of joint. But he knew that he had nothing to gain and a lot to lose if he showed his feelings. He was determined that he was going to marry Barbara come what may, and he had his own ideas of what their future plans were going to be. So he decided to go along with all the ideas Harriet and Barbara discussed. He was still apprehensive about the visit to the solicitor in the near future, and hoped there would be no major drawbacks in getting control of Barbara's wealth. He still had no idea how much money was entailed, or what were the conditions of her inheritance. He just hoped that it would all be straightforward. He realised that Harriet would try to protect her great-niece from being hurt, and that he was going to have to be very careful.

He left about eleven, having seen that Harriet was beginning to look tired after all the excitement. He, too, wished to have some time to himself, to mull over his future plans. As he drove back to Minehead he felt a glow of satisfaction. His future was beginning to look bright.

Chapter 13

Over the next few months Harriet and Barbara were kept busy. They made an appointment to see Mr McGrath, the solicitor in charge of both their affairs. He was a small middle-aged man with a bushy moustache, bright intelligent eyes, and a Scottish accent that almost thirty years in England had not erased. He had studied law at Oxford and could have become a barrister, but he preferred the quiet life in the west of England. He had fallen in love while at Oxford, with a Taunton girl whose father was a lawyer in the town, and who had been happy to have his son-in-law join the firm. Mr McGrath returned to Speyside every year for two weeks' fishing, but was content with his practice and his wife and family. He was a kindly soul.

"Yes, Miss Morris," he said, with a friendly smile, "I can easily make arrangements for the house in West Mallet to be sold. In fact I'm sure the Cathedral would be happy to buy it. Mind you, you'd probably get more for it on the open market, but let me sound things out for you. Now about the money you'll get from it. What do you want to do with it? You say your fiancé is now working in Taunton, so I presume you'll want to buy something in the district."

"Of course," said Barbara. "We want something that could take my parent's furniture. I don't want a modern house. We would rather buy an old house. Then we can modernise it ourselves. Philip has some novel ideas which he'd like to carry out."

"This is Philip Sharp I gather. He has just moved to the Western Bank branch here, hasn't he? I've heard about him" said Mr McGrath. "Anyway, leave it with me and I'll get back to you when I have a better idea of how much you'll probably get from the house. The market is good just now."

He turned to Harriet. "Now Mrs Tremayne, can I have a few minutes of your time please?"

This was a hint to Barbara to leave her great-aunt alone with the solicitor. "I'll go and do some shopping, and meet you in the car park in about half an hour. Thank you, Mr McGrath, for your time and advice."

The door shut behind Barbara and there was a pause before Mr McGrath spoke to Harriet. "Now, Mrs Tremayne, tell me what's bothering you. I gathered from your phone call that it's something to do with Barbara marrying this Sharp fellow."

"Yes it is. I have a feeling that although he says he loves Barbara, he also loves the money she will bring him. Is there any way we can tie up what she gets from the sale of the house? I know he has suggested buying the house himself with the help of a mortgage from the bank. But I'll just feel uneasy if Barbara gets all the capital from the West Mallet house. I've heard that he's a clever investor and accountant, but I've also heard a rumour that he's inclined to take risks with the investments. I would hate Barbara to be the loser."

Putting his hands together and leaning his elbows on the desk, Mr McGrath thought for a moment. He then gave a slight grunt and said, "Hmm. How would it be if they found a house they liked, and we arranged for them to buy it? But in Barbara's name only, and in trust for any children she would have. In this day and age there are so many divorces that this would be to protect Barbara from being made homeless. I expect Sharp will probably protest, but I think if he does, then it will prove he's only marrying her for her money. Does he know that she doesn't receive control of her main inheritance until she is thirty five?"

"Yes, he does. Barbara has been very open about it all, and as I've said, he seems to give the impression that he doesn't care about the money. But I'm sure he does. Am I being a nasty, suspicious old woman?"

"No, my dear lady. You are not. When they are in the process of buying the new house we'll have him in for a consultation and then we'll see how things go. As one of the Trustees, of course, you'll have to be present too. I'm sure we can arrange something to protect Barbara's inheritance. I, too, have heard that Mr Sharp is supposed to be a bit clever at taking risks with the investments. Maybe we are just getting a bit cynical about people these days. But it's better to be safe isn't it?"

"I sincerely hope so. I know I can trust you to help me. Now I've taken up enough of your time."

They shook hands and Harriet made her way out of the office. She paused at the top of the steps. She suddenly felt very old. She shook her head and told herself not to be silly, as she stepped slowly down to the pavement and across to the car park. She found her great-niece had had a splendid time shopping for her trousseau. The back seat of the car was crowded with bags. "If you go on spending like this my girl you'll be bankrupt before you even get up the aisle," Harriet remarked.

Barbara laughed at her great-aunt. "I'll only get married once, and I intend to enjoy it."

"These days, people seem to forget their marriage vows almost immediately," Harriet said.

"That's not going to happen to us. You are an old misery today, Aunt Harriet. Come on. It's supposed to be a happy time for us all. After all, you are getting rid of the responsibility for me. You've put up with me long enough. Bless you." She leaned across and kissed Harriet on the cheek.

By the middle of March the West Mallet house had been sold to the Cathedral Commissioners and they had agreed to allow

Barbara to continue to store her parents' furniture until she had acquired her new house. Mr McGrath had obtained an excellent price for the house and had invested the money short term in a building society.

The couple were beginning to despair of ever finding a house they both liked. But at the beginning of April Barbara received a phone call from Philip saying that he'd heard of a house for sale on the outskirts of Taunton, on the Wellington Road. He'd made an appointment for them to view it that evening. Could she come and see it with him at five o'clock?

"Yes. I'll meet you, and perhaps we can have dinner afterwards. Oh, I do hope this will be the one. I seem to have seen so many, and none of them were right were they? See you later darling."

At five o'clock they were outside a detached double-fronted house with large bay windows and a glass-fronted porch. The particulars said the house had been built in 1911, and it looked in good repair. The agent showed them over it. There was a large hall with the stairs going up the right hand side to a small landing, before continuing up to another large hall. The two rooms in the front downstairs were large, with high ceilings with classical mouldings and a centre rose which held the main light. Behind was a breakfast room, off which was the kitchen. There was an old-fashioned black range, which Barbara decided should be replaced by an Aga. The sitting room was large, with a moulded ceiling and glass doors which opened on to a balcony, with steps leading down to a mature garden at the back. Upstairs were four bedrooms and a bathroom, plus a small box room which held an airing cupboard. Stairs led up to two attic rooms. Ideal for a playroom, thought Barbara. There was also a basement with plenty of room for storage. A garage had also been erected at the side of the house.

"Perhaps it is too big for a young couple," said the agent,

"But it should be a good investment, and it is within your price range."

"Yes. I agree, don't you Philip? It's exactly the kind of house I'd like to live in."

"Mr Stracey," said Philip, "We'd like to discuss this and get back to you. But I rather think that Miss Morris has decided she likes it. Can I get in touch with you tomorrow and let you know our decision."

"Of course, Mr Sharp. But I wouldn't leave it too long as it is a well-built house and there are other people who want to view it. The owner wants a quick sale, too. His wife died recently and he intends going to live with his son in Gloucester."

Mr Stracey left them in the driveway. Barbara grabbed hold of Philip's hand and rushed him round to the back of the house to have another look, and to inspect the garden.

"Oh, Philip darling. It's just exactly what I want. We can modernise it. The bathroom is a bit tacky, and that range will have to come out. But it has such possibilities hasn't it?"

"My love, don't you think it's a bit big for us? I know it is lovely, but do we need such a large house just yet?" Secretly, he too loved the house, and could imagine how impressed his colleagues at the bank would be. It would certainly enhance his reputation. He also knew that he could afford it if he let Barbara buy it. He felt he had to remind her that he could put down a deposit, and get a mortgage from the bank. But he hoped that she would insist on paying for it outright.

"Let's discuss it over dinner, and then we'll tell Aunt Harriet, and see what she thinks, shall we?" Barbara was as excited as a small child going to a party.

Philip was getting a trifle annoyed with Barbara insisting on asking Harriet's advice all the time, and could hardly wait until they were married, when he hoped Harriet's influence would wane. Hiding his annoyance, he went along with

Barbara's suggestion.

Barbara had taken the bus from Minehead into Taunton, so Philip drove her back to Stickleburn immediately after dinner, so that they could tell Harriet all about the house. In front of the sitting room fire they sat and talked, while Harriet listened. Philip attempted to protest when Harriet suggested that Barbara bought the house. He was pleased, until he learned that Mr McGrath would be in charge of negotiating and buying, and that Harriet would make arrangements for a consultation with the solicitor, for them all to thrash out the details. It was decided that Harriet would get in touch with Mr McGrath in the morning and instruct him to put in an offer for the house, subject to having a survey done. Philip again felt annoyance at having the decision and arrangements taken out of his hands. Inwardly he was furious. He didn't stay long afterwards, making the excuse that he had a busy day ahead of him. Barbara felt he was a bit abrupt as he kissed her goodnight. Perhaps he was just tired. At least she hoped so.

She was too excited to sleep, and lay for a long time thinking and planning the alterations that they would make to the house. Her brain was too active for sleep, so she put the light on and fetched a drawing pad from her desk. She started to sketch out the layout of the house, and plan the bathroom and kitchen. She wanted both rooms to be light and airy. She could picture just where her parents' furniture would go, and longed to get everything out of store. Eventually she fell asleep with the light still on, and woke up in the morning feeling happy and exhilarated.

Two days later, they all met in Mr McGrath's office, and he put forward the suggestion that the house would be in Barbara's name alone, with the proviso that it should be entailed for any children of the marriage. Harriet noticed that Philip was not ecstatic about this.

"It is safeguarding Barbara, and any children you may

have," explained Mr McGrath. "If, by any chance, you were killed, it would mean that your wife and family would be safe financially."

Philip forbore to point out that with Barbara's inheritance at thirty-five, she would certainly always be financially secure. However, he decided discretion was called for, and agreed. He also knew his own capital was safe, and no requirement for a mortgage would mean that his salary would allow him to make further investments. His ambition was to set up as an accountant and investment advisor on his own. Banking was simply a means to an end, and he knew he had the ability to be a success. He liked taking risks, especially with other people's money, and making a profit for them and, of course, for himself.

Chapter 14

The wedding was set to take place towards the end of July. Somehow, with Harriet's knowledge of the local builders and decorators, the house was ready for occupation by the end of June. Arrangements were made for the removal of the furniture stored in the West Mallet house. Barbara was delighted when she saw that her parents' furniture was just what the house required.

She insisted that the front room on the left of the hall was to be Philip's study and library. Her father's old knee-hole desk was placed in the bay window, and his green leather chairs sat at either side of the fireplace. Shelves had been built into the alcoves, and her father's books of classical writers were once again on display. She spent a long time arranging them to her satisfaction. An antique bookcase with a cupboard underneath was placed opposite the fireplace. She left it vacant for any books that Philip might have. When he saw the finished room, Philip was surprised at her perception, and at how imaginative she had been. It was a room for a gentleman, exactly what he had envisaged for himself if ever he could have afforded it. He was grateful to her. His face was a picture of delight and he flung his arms round her and swung her off her feet to express his pleasure.

The rest of the house came together as if by magic. Curtains which had hung in the old house had been cleaned and were now in the dining room and most of the bedrooms. New green and cream regency-striped curtains framed the study windows, and blue brocade curtains hung either side of the windows and glass doors of the sitting room.

The bathroom had been completely renovated with cream tiles on the walls, and a cream bath and washbasin were installed. The builder had suggested that as the room was so big, they could make a separate lavatory with a washbasin in it as well. An Aga replaced the old black range in the kitchen and there was an electric cooker as well. Oil-fired central heating was also put in at Philip's suggestion, and the whole house blossomed with new paint and paper.

Philip was rapidly becoming used to the idea that his ambitions and dreams were about to come true, and he dreaded to think that anything could happen to mar his feeling of complacency. His love for Barbara deepened, although he still would not give way to his passion. He knew that Barbara's wishes to wait until they were married must be kept. It was hard for both of them at times. He, at least, could get sexual satisfaction when he occasionally went up to Bristol at the weekends to see his parents. One of his old girlfriends, whose husband was in the army in Korea, welcomed him to her arms and bed. Both knew it was for their mutual satisfaction. Philip didn't feel guilt at all. His feelings for Barbara were completely separate, and he was careful not to antagonise Harriet. He realised how much depended on her approval. Her great-niece had been her responsibility for the last six years, and he knew how much affection there was between them.

Once they were married and settled in their new home it would be different. Life would be so much easier for him. However, he knew that he had to tread warily with Harriet at present. His parents and his sister Mary and her family were coming down for the wedding. Mary and the family were booked in to stay in bed and breakfast accommodation in Porlock, while Harriet had booked his parents into the Northcliffe Hotel for the weekend, and had arranged transport to be laid on to take them to the church and reception and back to the hotel. She said to Philip that she would make sure they were well looked after for the whole weekend. They were a quiet couple who were happiest in their own home.

The day of the wedding dawned misty, but with the promise that it would clear later. The marquee had been erected with a special canopy leading from the sitting room patio door; just in case it rained. The local florist, under Harriet's supervision, had decorated the marquee and the tables with orange, cream and yellow flowers, which was echoed in the embroidery on the one bridesmaid's dress. Jane Hart, Barbara's friend from school, now with a law degree behind her, was to be the bridesmaid. They had always been firm friends. Jane was about to embark on her ambition to be a barrister. She had found great opposition amongst the male applicants for places for her year's pupilage, but was confident she could compete with them on an equal footing.

"I'm not really a feminist," she'd told Barbara the previous evening, "But I don't see why there should be a closed shop against female barristers. I want to specialise in cases of rape and wife battering, and who better to defend the victims?"

Barbara agreed. "Well I'll know who to come to if Philip ever becomes violent."

"He'd better not," replied Jane. "He's really dishy isn't he? But I get the impression he's the dominant type, so make sure you hold your own with him."

"Are you girls ready?" Harriet entered Barbara's room. "Come on, it's time we were all dressed. The cars will be here soon. In fact, Jane's parents have just arrived to pick her up. My word you do look lovely in that dress, Jane."

The full skirted dress was of cream *broderie anglaise* with orange and yellow flowers and green foliage. Similar coloured flowers were arranged in her hair band. Barbara wore her mother's wedding dress of ivory silk with the skirt cut on the bias, which clung to the bride's slim figure. The veil was edged with Honiton lace, and had actually been worn first by Barbara's grandmother.

Harriet's eyes moistened as she looked at her great-niece.

She remembered that she and her sister wore that veil almost fifty years previously. Barbara had so many mannerisms that reminded Harriet of those happy days. She had been fifteen when she had been bridesmaid to her sister. A world gone by, never to return. Barbara looked radiant. Harriet went across to her, handing her the bouquet of cream and yellow roses. She kissed her cheek before placing the veil over her face. "Dearest Barbara. You look beautiful. All I ever wish for you is your happiness. Now come on, girls. It's time we left."

The lovely little church at Luccombe was packed. It was unusual to have the bride given away by her great-aunt, but it had been Barbara's wish. Harriet felt very proud as she walked slowly up the aisle to stand in front of the vicar. Her one regret was that Annette and John were not part of the ceremony. Philip looked resplendent in his morning coat. His best man was a colleague from the bank. As Barbara reached him, he turned to look at her. She was so lovely that the sight almost took his breath away.

Once the ceremony was over and the photographs taken outside the church, the young couple were driven back to Stickleburn for the reception. Philip kissed Barbara gently as they arrived at the cottage and whispered, "Thank God that's over, Mrs Sharp. I can't wait till we can get away to Bath. The reception won't go on too long, will it?"

"Darling, we can't rush away too soon. It would be impolite. But surely we can get away before five. That should give us plenty of time to get to Bath before dinner."

"It's not dinner I'm after and well you know it. Oh hell, here comes Harriet and the parents."

The reception passed in a blur for Barbara. They shook hands with all the guests, and then sat down for the wedding feast. Neither of them had much appetite for the delicious meal which was served. Philip drank sufficient champagne to get him through the speeches and the cutting of the cake. He realised that he had better have a few cups of black coffee to sober him up before driving off with Barbara.

At 4.30 Barbara went upstairs with Jane to change out of her wedding dress into her going-away outfit, a beautiful blue linen dress with an edge-to-edge coat to match. On her head was a small blue straw hat. She had gone with Aunt Harriet to London to get the outfit, a Norman Hartnell design. Harriet was determined her one and only niece should have the best.

Philip had changed in the guest bedroom and was waiting for her at the foot of the stairs. She came softly down, carrying her bouquet, and smiled at the assembled guests waiting by the car in the drive. Philip held the car door open for her and, as she was about to get in, she tossed her bouquet high, laughing as she did. Jane was the lucky one to catch it. Waving it like a flag, she rushed to hug Barbara. Philip got behind the wheel, and with a clatter of tin cans he drove down the drive, turned left on to the road and quickly disappeared.

Jane ran back to where Harriet stood looking rather forlorn. She hugged her and took her arm as they went back into the house. "Aunt Harriet," she said, "I think I'd like to place these flowers on Mr and Mrs Morris's grave when I get back to West Mallet tomorrow. They would have been so proud of what you've done for Barbara."

"Jane you are a dear. Let's have another glass of champagne, and then I'd better circulate round the guests before they start to move off. Thank God, you're staying the night with me. Tomorrow I'll be sane again. I just hope she'll be happy, bless her."

"So do I. I can't say I'm all that enamoured of him though. Not my type. Oh dear, perhaps I shouldn't have said that."

"No, I'm glad you did. I was wary of him at first. I think it's just his manner." She smiled. "He improves as you get to know him."

Chapter 15

Philip pulled the car into a lay-by as soon as he could, took off his jacket, and then untied the tin cans. Barbara got out of the car, took off her hat and coat, shaking the confetti out of them, before flinging them onto the back seat. They laughed as they got back into the car.

"Thank the Lord it's all over and we're now on our own at last," said Barbara.

Philip pulled her into his arms and kissed her passionately, before switching on the engine again. He drove off in the direction of Bath, where they were to spend the first night of their honeymoon.

The hotel on the outskirts of Bath was a lovely old manor house which had been converted into a luxury hotel. Their room had large windows, overlooking a terraced garden with a shimmering lake in the distance. It was richly furnished, with an enormous four-poster bed with deep red brocade curtains. Barbara blushed as she looked at Philip, who smiled broadly at her.

Once the porter had been tipped and closed the door behind him, Philip came towards her and putting his arms around her, laid his face against hers and said softly, "I think we should have dinner early, my love. Then we can have an early night. You must be tired. I know I feel bushed. Just think Mrs Sharp, we have ten whole days in which to be together. I love you dearly. Go and powder your nose and we'll go down for dinner now. I'm hungry. I wasn't at the reception – I was just too nervous – and I noticed you hardly ate anything either."

"Yes, I'm famished too. I was too excited and nervous to eat much earlier. In fact the reception is just a blur to me. Apart from seeing Aunt Harriet almost in tears before we left.

I think she was just happy for me. She's been an angel."

"Well, she's certainly pulled out all the stops to make the wedding go well." said Philip.

Over dinner in the restaurant they talked of the day's happenings, laughing over some of the amusing things that had been said or done. Both agreed that Mary's children were rumbustious and needed a bit more discipline. Young Roger, aged ten, bored with all the speeches had wandered into the garden, and climbed one of the tall beech trees that grew in a corner. However, he discovered once he'd got up that he didn't have the nerve to try and clamber down. A crow perched on the topmost branch flew off in alarm, showering Roger with white excreta. His angry and frightened cries had finally penetrated the hub of conversation in the marquee, and someone had fetched a ladder to bring the child down. Everyone had laughed at the sight of the bedraggled boy covered in white. He had not been amused, and had been hustled into the cottage bathroom, where his shirt had been stripped off him and washed out. His dignity was impaired, and it was a chastened young lad who rejoined the company, wearing an old jumper of Barbara's.

Neither of them stayed for coffee after dinner. As they made their way up to their room, Philip told his new wife that he had a surprise waiting for her. He had secreted a bottle of champagne from the reception in his luggage, and it was cooling in the washbasin. Fetching two glasses from the en-suite bathroom, he quickly opened the bottle, and poured the golden coloured nectar into the glasses. Handing one to Barbara he said, "Here's to us, my darling. I hope I can make you a good husband, but you've taken me for better or worse. I pray it is for better."

"I love you, you silly man. Of course it is for better," answered Barbara.

They sipped the champagne slowly, smiling at each other.

Philip put both empty glasses down on the dressing table. Drawing Barbara into his arms, he gently undid the zip at the back of her dress and slipped it from her shoulders. His hands moved over her body. Undoing her bra, his kisses became passionate and he then let his lips caress her neck, before beginning to kiss her breasts. Barbara moaned softly, and her fingers started to undo the buttons of his shirt. Soon they were both standing naked and Philip bent to lift Barbara on to the bed. He climbed on to the bed beside her and his hands and lips roved over her body. She was filled with desire, and felt his hardness press against her. She opened her legs to him and he gently moved on top of her. She gave a little cry as he entered her, but then was lost in the pleasure of his lovemaking. They climaxed together and she gave a contented sigh as she relaxed.

"Oh darling, that was wonderful. Now I really feel married."

"Practice makes perfect, my love. Just give me a little time to recover and we can try again. Let's have some more champagne."

He wandered off into the bathroom to collect the bottle, and soon they were lying on the bed sipping from their glasses. His free hand roamed over her breasts, and she let her hand caress his chest. Feeling a bit daring, she let her hand wander down toward his groin, and was amazed to find that in a very short time he was aroused again. This time he embraced Barbara and pulled her on top of him. When he entered her this time, he also sucked at her nipples. Soon they were riding the heights, and it wasn't long before they were exhausted by their lovemaking. Waking up later in the night in the cradle of his arms, she felt that she had never been so happy.

Chapter 16

Ten days later they returned to Taunton and moved into their new home, having had an ecstatic time on their honeymoon in Wales. Barbara had never been there and Philip proved to be a fount of knowledge, as his mother was half Welsh. He had always taken a keen interest in its history and in his Celtic ancestry. They had made their base in a small hotel in Llandrindod Wells and from there they'd explored the countryside of the Brecon Beacons and the Black Mountains. The weather had been kind to them, and they returned tanned, fit and happy.

Barbara delighted in being a housewife, and loved planning the garden, which had been overgrown when they'd taken possession of the house. There was an old neglected rose garden at the end of the lawn, and she took great pleasure in weeding it and attempting to get it into some sort of order.

In the evenings when Philip came home from the bank, there was a beautifully cooked meal waiting to be served. His feelings as he entered the now lovely house were of security. He thought of it as his house, forgetting that it was in Barbara's name and entailed for any children they may have. As the summer gave way to autumn and then to winter, he loved returning to the warmth which enfolded him as he entered the front door.

Harriet came once a month to have lunch with Barbara, and if she had to come into Taunton on business, she invariably dropped in to see her great-niece. As these visits were usually during the day, Philip didn't see much of her, which suited him very well. Occasionally on a Sunday they would drive out to Stickleburn.

At the end of November, Barbara suspected that she might be pregnant, but decided that she wouldn't tell Philip until she was certain. She made an appointment to see her doctor two weeks before Christmas, and he confirmed her suspicions. She thought she would wait until Christmas Eve to tell Philip, just before his parents arrived to spend three days over the festive season, with their son and his new wife. Harriet was going to drive over on Christmas Day.

Barbara spent a lot of time and her own money in decorating the tree in the hall. She also bought Philip a modern electric typewriter that she knew he wanted. Just the right thing for his desk in the study, which they used more as a sitting room when they were on their own. It was a cosy and comfortable room, especially in the winter.

Philip came home at lunch on Christmas Eve. The bank had closed until after Boxing Day. The delicious aroma of baking filled the house, and he entered the kitchen to find Barbara taking her second batch of mince pies out of the oven. She had obviously spent the morning preparing for her visitors. Putting the tins down on to the wooden boards, she turned round to greet her husband.

"Oh Babs," he laughed, "You've got flour on your nose and in your hair, and your cheeks are glowing. Come on, let's sit down for a few minutes before we have some of your soup. I'll get us a couple of glasses of sherry. It's our first Christmas in our own home. Isn't it wonderful? I love you dearly." He leaned forward said kissed her floury nose.

He went to get the sherry, and Barbara was glad to sit down. She'd been very sick that morning, after Philip had gone to work. Luckily it didn't last long, but she'd felt rotten for half an hour. She hoped this phase of her pregnancy would soon be over.

Philip returned to the kitchen with the glasses of sherry on a small silver tray. "Happy Christmas, darling," he said, as he handed her a glass and sat himself down at the table.

"Happy Christmas to you Philip. Next year we'll have

another member of the family in the house."

A puzzled look appeared on his face. "Who?" he asked, looking at her. Then he understood what she was trying to tell him. "Good Lord! When did you know? I'm delighted darling. How about you? Are you all correct?"

"Of course I am," she laughed. "Dr Reid confirmed it last Tuesday. But I thought I'd spring it on you today."

He hugged her to him. Just what he had wanted. He felt even more secure, knowing they were about to have a child. He was becoming more possessive about the house than before. He realised that he had to be extremely careful not to reveal what he felt about the house to anyone. True, he loved Barbara, and the novelty of being married had not worn off. He was thrilled about the baby, secure in his knowledge that it would strengthen the marriage.

After a snack lunch, he insisted on washing up the dishes while Barbara had a short rest, before they drove to the station to pick up his parents. It was a crisp sunny winter's day, and the trees in the garden were etched black against the blue of the sky. The holly bush at the side of the house was covered in red berries. The previous Sunday he'd cut some small pieces to use as decoration in the hall. He'd managed to buy Barbara an antique silver and blue enamel butterfly brooch with amber eyes as his present to her. It had cost him more than he'd intended to spend, but he was now glad that he'd taken it.

At three o'clock he took a cup of tea up to the bedroom for her. She was sound asleep under the quilt, and looked so peaceful that he hated to wake her up. But they wanted to go together to meet his parents, and would tell them about the baby at supper time. He knew they would be impressed by the house, which they'd not seen yet.

Barbara was slightly apprehensive about the arrival of Philip's parents. She felt that she'd been unable to find a common bond with his mother, a small plump woman with grey hair and slate grey eyes, which gave her a cold steely look. His father was tall, with salt and pepper hair with a red tinge to it. His brown eyes gave out a warmth which Barbara found endearing. He was a strong silent man, but his wife made up for his quietness. As soon as she entered the house she exclaimed, "Well Philip, you've done nicely for yourself, haven't you? Mind you, I can't say I'd like to live with all this old furniture. But I suppose it would cost a fair bit to buy these days. That is if you like that sort of thing."

Barbara felt her hackles rise, and longed to say that if Meg Sharp didn't like it, she could go home on the next train. But Philip had warned her that his mother was forthright and blunt, and not to take offence. So she smiled sweetly at her mother-in-law, and turning to Philip, asked him, "Will you show your parents over the house while I attend to supper? It should be ready in about half an hour. We can have a drink beforehand."

Jack Sharp looked at his daughter-in-law, and smiled apologetically. "I'll look forward to that drink, Barbara. It's grand to be here for Christmas. That's an appetising smell coming from the kitchen."

"What would you like to drink, Father? We have beer, sherry or whisky."

"I'd love a glass of whisky, and Meg will take sweet sherry if you have it."

He followed his son and wife upstairs, and Barbara went through to the kitchen, pleased that she had some rapport with her father-in-law, but still prickly about her mother-in-law. "Thank God they're only here for three days," she said softly to the cat, lying in his basket by the Aga, "I only hope she's not going to make any more snide remarks."

She checked that the casserole was cooking, and then went

into the dining-room to pour the drinks. She felt she could do with a large glass of sherry before they all descended, but knew that she had to keep her wits about her. She'd realised before the wedding that Philip was his mother's favourite, and that she had resented Barbara when she'd visited them in Bristol. However, she was on Barbara's territory now, and although Philip was still her son, he was also Barbara's husband, and she had to realise that his home was now here.

After supper Meg rose smartly and started to clear the table before Philip and his father had finished their wine.

"Mother," Philip protested, "We've not finished yet. Please leave the dishes just now. I'll help Barbara with them later."

"No, you won't, lad," she replied rather sharply, "While I'm here I'll help with the dishes."

"Will you please sit down, Mother," said Philip sternly, "We have something to tell you, and we can't do it with you hovering around."

His mother was rather taken aback at his tone, and sat down as she was told.

Philip continued, "In July, you are to be grandparents again. That is what we want you to know. We are delighted and we hope you will be too."

Jack beamed at Barbara, and raised his glass. "Congratulations. I'm delighted, and I'm sure Mother is too."

"Well, it didn't take you long did it?" Meg said stonily.

"There is no need to make remarks like that," her husband rebuked her.

The atmosphere in the room became rather chilly, and in an effort to defuse it Barbara said, "Why don't we go through to the sitting room to have our coffee, and Philip will pour you a glass of liqueur. After all it is Christmas Eve and we have to celebrate." She got up from the table, and made her way to the kitchen to make the coffee. Through the hatch, she saw her mother-in-law say something to Philip as he led her out of the dining room. He glared at his mother, and Barbara heard him say to her, "Just watch what you say, Mother. I don't want Barbara upset."

The rest of the evening passed pleasantly enough, although Mrs Sharp looked as if she were sitting on eggshells. Luckily, about ten o'clock she announced that she was going to bed, and that Jack had better not be long in following her. Barbara relaxed when Meg exited the room. She picked up the coffee tray and excused herself. Once in the kitchen, she started tidying up. Then she cleared the dining room. Before she started on the dishes, Philip came in to help her, and Jack came to the door.

"Goodnight Barbara," he said, smiling. "It is really good to be with you this Christmas. The meal was delicious. Philip's a lucky lad to have found himself such an excellent wife. Sleep well, dear."

Chapter 17

Next morning Barbara was wakened by Philip, who brought her a cup of tea and a sweet biscuit. She felt a bit queasy, but was told by Philip that he'd heard from one of his colleagues that this was one way to combat morning sickness, and that she hadn't to get up yet. It was only seven, and they'd told his parents breakfast would be at eight-thirty.

"I've taken Mother and Father a tray of tea as well," he told her, "That'll keep them happy until then."

He got back into bed, and after drinking the tea and nibbling the biscuit, they cuddled down together. With Philip's arms around her, Barbara felt warm and content. She rather wished they were on their own and could spend more time in bed, but she knew she had to get up and dressed soon, to go and prepare breakfast.

On reaching the kitchen, she discovered that Philip had already set the dining room table for the meal, so all she had to do was prepare breakfast. She felt so lucky that she had a caring and loving husband.

Her mother-in-law came into the kitchen as Barbara was frying the bacon. She carried the tray and her hot water bottle was tucked under her arm. "Good morning Barbara," she said, "I trust you slept well. I hope you're not going to suffer bad morning sickness. It really makes you feel rotten. I remember when I was expecting Philip it went on for months. I wasn't so bad with the girls, but I did crave sour eating apples. It's funny the fads we women get when pregnant."

"Meg!" boomed a voice from the hall, "Leave the poor girl in peace first thing in the morning, can't you? We're not all like you, nattering all the time."

"Jack Sharp, I don't natter all the time."

"Come into the dining room. It's all set for breakfast and I can smell the bacon."

Barbara smiled to herself. She felt grateful to her father-in-law in removing his wife from the kitchen.

After breakfast was cleared, they decided to open their presents. Barbara was thrilled with her brooch and Philip was surprised and excited with his typewriter. The Sharps Senior had got them a crystal jug and glasses.

"They really are lovely," said Barbara, "We'll use them today for the Christmas dinner. Thank you so much." She gave both the parents a hug.

Meg Sharp was a slightly taken aback by the warmth of the hug, and was rather pleased. Underneath her brittle exterior there was a woman who loved her family, and responded to the affection shown to her. She'd been a nursing sister, and was accustomed to ordering her staff around. She'd tried it at home, but it didn't work with Jack.

Once the present-opening was over Barbara asked if everyone would like coffee. Meg at once offered to help, and this time Barbara was grateful for her assistance. The two women worked well in the kitchen together, and soon everything was under control for the Christmas meal, which was timed for one thirty.

Great Aunt Harriet arrived about twelve, and produced a bottle of champagne, which they decided to open before the meal.

Meg had been a bit apprehensive at meeting Harriet again. She'd felt a bit intimidated by her at the wedding, and realised that she'd met her match. She needed to be on her guard if she was going to hold her own with Harriet. But after a glass of champagne she felt more mellow.

The turkey was deliciously tender, and the pudding rich with fruit. Philip carried it in ceremoniously, with a sprig of holly on top and blazing with brandy that Barbara lit just as he was about to enter the dining room. Meg was quite subdued after the meal. She sat in her chair drowsily beaming at everyone. The pre-dinner drinks and the wine with the meal had obviously affected her. Even Jack noticed it, and smiled at the assembled company, "I'll know what to do in future when she starts to nag me. Just give her a good slug of sherry."

"To hear you talk, you would think I was a bad-tempered old hag, Jack Sharp," Meg retorted. "I'm not, am I, Philip?"

"No Mum. Underneath that stern exterior there's just an old softy. I love you anyway."

Her smile became even broader. "Well someone appreciates me."

It was a happy family evening. Harriet left about eight o'clock. She'd really enjoyed herself, but was beginning to feel tired. She and Meg had helped with the washing up and so everything was tidy. Barbara was glad the day had been successful. Her first Christmas in her own home as a married woman had proved a very happy occasion.

Boxing Day was quiet. Meg was a bit subdued. She complained of a headache, and was teased about having a hangover. She took it in good spirit. But she decided not to join the others when they went for a walk. She would just have a rest. Supper that night consisted of cold ham and turkey, with salad and left-over trifle, and the atmosphere was relaxed.

The next day, Jack and Meg departed, and Barbara felt guilty as she gave a sigh of relief. She was glad their first visit was over, and now she understood that her mother-in-law had been just as nervous as she had.

Chapter 18

During the next few months, Philip was a devoted father-to-be. Barbara felt cherished and loved. As July approached, she felt that she looked like a very pregnant cow, and suffered a lot from heartburn. She was more than relieved one evening towards the end of July to begin experiencing labour pains. Philip, in a panic, took her to the nursing home as quickly as he could. He kept pacing the corridor until the rather buxom Matron told him to go home. "You're just getting in the way of the staff, and at any rate it'll be quite some time before your wife goes into the final stages of labour. You're worrying unnecessarily. Please go home and try to relax. We'll phone you once it's all over."

He was rather glad to be breathing fresh air as he came out of the door. He climbed into the car and drove home, where he poured himself a stiff whisky and then went to bed.

At six o'clock the following morning he was wakened by the telephone ringing downstairs, and rushed to answer it. "Mr Sharp, your wife has just given birth to a son, who weighed in at eight pounds, three ounces. If you wish to see them both on your way to work, please call in. Both are well, but Mrs Sharp is a bit tired."

"Thank you," he replied, "I'll be there as soon as I can. It's wonderful news. Give them my love."

He was really thrilled. He felt exhilarated too, as he knew that his financial position was much stronger, now that he had a son. Always at the back of his mind was the thought that one day he would be able to gain control of Barbara's money. If only he could get the entailment clause cancelled. But he knew that, for the time being, he must be extremely cautious. He cut some of the roses from the garden. Later he would buy Barbara a special present. But it was far too early for the flower shop to be open.

By seven he was back at the nursing home, and was shown into the room where Barbara lay, white-faced and tired against the pillows. She was holding the baby in her arms, and smiled wearily at Philip as he entered. Placing the roses on the bedside cabinet, he leaned over and kissed her tenderly on the brow. "Aren't you a clever girl? Bless you darling. Are you very tired and was it terrible? I didn't sleep much, as I kept hoping the phone would ring. How is our son? Can I hold him?"

"So many questions, Philip. It was painful towards the end, but it was worth it. Here you are darling. David John Sharp, meet your father." She gently placed the sleeping babe in his arms.

Philip looked down on the small red-faced baby with a look of pride and wonder. At that moment he thought he'd never been so happy in all his life. He was silent for some time before he realised that he really hadn't taken much notice of his wife. Handing the child back to Barbara, he bent again and kissed her on her lips, and softly touched her face. "Thank you darling. I do love you so much, and now we have this little chap to love as well. You must rest as much as possible. I'm so proud of you."

A few minutes late Sister McKenzie entered and said sternly, "I think your wife could do with some rest Mr Sharp. Off you go, and come back this evening, when she'll have perked up a bit. She had a long labour and is very tired."

As he left, Barbara asked him to let Aunt Harriet and his parents know of the safe arrival of their son.

"I was going to, darling. See you later. Is there anything you need?"

Barbara shook her head and handed David John Sharp to the sister, who placed him in the cot at the side of her bed.

Ten days later Barbara arrived home with the baby, who had gained weight steadily since his birth. She'd had a couple of days when she was weepy and depressed, but was positively glowing when she arrived home. She had quickly regained her figure, although her breasts were fuller. She insisted on feeding him herself. She'd read the Truby King book beforehand, and decided to go with the advice given, that it was better for both mother and child. She enjoyed the time she spent with him as he suckled. Sometimes her breasts were so full and hard that it was a relief when he sucked until he fell asleep.

He was a placid baby, and soon grew into a happy smiling child, who, by the time he was one, had already taken his first steps. Both parents doted on him, and Aunt Harriet often called just for the joy of seeing him. She often said to Barbara that he was so like her father, and that if he inherited his nature, he would be a very lucky child. This announcement didn't exactly please Philip much. However, he was always careful to keep on the right side of Harriet. He knew better than to antagonise her.

His work at the bank had expanded and, as he had foreseen, his own savings had increased. He was a shrewd investor, and through his business connections he learned that a firm of accountants in Taunton were looking for a new partner. Samuel Peterson, one of the partners in Mead, Jones and Peterson approached him one evening in the Conservative Club, which Philip had joined shortly after his marriage. "Philip, I hear that you're perhaps looking to branch into accountancy. Would you consider coming in with us? We could do with some new blood. Jerome Mead is thinking of retiring in a year or two. What do you say?"

"Well Sam, I'd have to think about it and discuss it with Barbara. I'd have to buy myself in, wouldn't I? I'm not sure whether I've got enough capital. How much do you think I'll need?"

Sam mentioned a sum, in excess of what Philip had in mind. Poker-faced, he said, "May I think about it and get back to you?"

"Certainly you may. Tell you what. Think about it over the weekend and come and see me on Tuesday at four-thirty."

"Fine. And thank you Sam for thinking of me. I've been hoping that something like this would come along soon. I feel I need the challenge."

Philip was very thoughtful over dinner that evening, and a puzzled Barbara looked carefully at him. "You seem worried about something, Philip. You're very quiet and thoughtful. Has anything happened to you today to upset you?"

"No. Not upset me. I met Sam Peterson at the Club, and he says they're looking for another partner. He asked if I was interested. Actually, I am very interested. It's just what I've always wanted. But they want more than I can afford, to become a partner. The opportunity is great, and I could double my salary at the bank. But I'm afraid I'll have to turn it down."

Philip knew that he had aroused Barbara's interest. Silence reigned for a minute and then she asked. "How much do you require to become a partner?"

Philip thought for a minute and then mentioned a sum in excess of what was required. If possible he didn't want to use all of his own savings.

Barbara rose from the table and walked round to where he sat. She put her arms round him and said with a smile. "I don't see any difficulty in raising that money. I can help you. Please, I'd like to. After all, it is for the benefit of us all isn't it?"

"I can't let you take the risk, darling. What if something goes wrong and I lose the lot?" he protested, knowing full well that she could easily afford to invest some money in him.

"You won't my love. I know how clever you are. Everyone is pleased with your work at the bank. What about your pension rights? Can you transfer them to the new firm?"

"Who is a bright girl? I must make enquiries about it. I am loth to take your money, but it really is a wonderful opportunity."

"Then it's settled, darling. I'll go and see Mr McGrath on Monday, and tell him to transfer the money to your account."

Philip hid his excitement from Barbara. He put his arms up and pulled her head down to his to kiss her passionately. He didn't feel guilty about exploiting her. His ambition came first.

Mr McGrath was disinclined to transfer so much of Barbara's money to Philip. He advised her against it, but she was adamant. He then insisted that Philip should sign a receipt for the money, which would be deposited with all Barbara's legal documents. He was quite sure that Mrs Tremayne would not be happy about the transaction. She had always been suspicious about Philip's aspirations. Barbara returned home triumphantly, and told Philip that the money would be his in a few days.

Chapter 19

Tuesday's meeting with Sam Peterson and his partners went well, and it was agreed that Philip would put in his resignation from the bank the next day. That would give him a month before he began as a partner in Meade, Jones and Peterson. The financial agreement would be drawn up, and all the partners would meet again to sign the partnership documents in two weeks' time.

A jubilant Philip arrived home that evening carrying a bottle of champagne. Barbara was in the kitchen, having just bathed David and got him ready for bed, when the front door was slammed shut.

"Darling, where are you? It's all settled. Isn't it wonderful news? We're going to celebrate tonight." Philip appeared in the doorway looking flushed and excited. He hurried over and soundly kissed his wife. Flourishing the bottle of champagne, he skipped to the refrigerator so that it could cool. Then he bent down, picked up his rosy faced son from his pen, and hugged him tightly saying in a joyful voice. "Your daddy is going to make his fortune. Aren't you a lucky boy to have such a clever daddy?"

David squealed with fright at the suddenness of being snatched from his pen where he'd been playing happily. His father thought it was funny, and threw him up in the air and caught him. David began to scream and cry. Tears were streaming down his little face. Barbara had to intervene and try and console him. "Darling, you've upset the child. He doesn't care to be snatched up like that. I know you're excited, but please, I was just keeping him quiet until you put him to bed."

Philip was furious that his moment of triumph had been spoiled. Barbara, who had been taken aback by his remark that he was so clever, was surprised by the look of anger on her husband's face. She felt that he'd overlooked the fact that, without her financial assistance, he wouldn't have got the partnership. But she didn't comment on it. She gently rocked David on her knee to quiet his sobs.

"You spoil that child. He'll grow up a cissy. He's got to be tough if he wants to succeed in life."

"Oh for heaven's sake, Philip, he's only a baby. Plenty of time to toughen him up when he goes to school." Barbara was beginning to be both annoyed and frightened by Philip's attitude. "Look," she said to him, "I'll take him up tonight. You go and get the champagne glasses. I'll be down in a few moments. We'll have the champagne before supper. We can eat when you're ready."

As she went upstairs carrying the now quiet baby, she thought she was seeing a side of Philip she'd not seen before. She wasn't sure she liked what she saw.

Philip, meanwhile, had time to reflect on his behaviour. He'd been so careful up until now. He knew that he had a temper that would engulf him at times, but felt he had it under control. He must defuse the situation and be apologetic when Barbara came back downstairs. He got the glasses out of the cupboard in the dining-room and took them into the sitting-room. Looking out at the garden, he noticed that the evening sun was causing long shadows of the trees across the lawn. The colourful display of roses and other pants soothed his anger, and when Barbara entered the room he turned to her saying, "Darling I'm so sorry. I've been anxious about this partnership so much that I've been tied up in knots in case something happened to prevent it. I do apologise for upsetting David. I didn't mean to. It was just the excitement. Please say you'll forgive me."

"Let's forget it shall we? Come on. Open up the bubbly and we can toast your successful future."

He struggled with the cork. Suddenly it went pop. Barbara had taken the precaution of having a glass at the ready, as the froth showered out of the bottle. With both glasses charged she handed one to Philip. "Good luck, Philip, with this new venture. It's what you've wanted isn't it? It will be to our advantage. Cheers, sweetheart."

The awkward feeling passed and by the time they had drunk the champagne and consumed their meal, the atmosphere had returned to normal.

Chapter 20

Three months later, Philip was truly settled as a partner with Mead, Jones and Peterson. Their offices were situated near the centre of Taunton. Philip's office was a fairly functional room with two large windows, which gave it plenty of light, but the décor was dingy.

"Philip," said Barbara, looking round the room, "You simply cannot work with those dull walls. It will have to have a lighter paper. I'll see if we can get someone to do it at a weekend And we'll have to take those curtains to be cleaned. They're grubby and dusty." She gave the curtains a pat and a cloud of dust was emitted into the room. "See what I mean? We can also get some paintings up on the walls. I think there are some of my grandfather's up in the attic. We can look when we get home."

In two weeks the room had undergone a complete transformation. The walls were covered with a cream paper with the woodwork painted to match. The cleaned curtains, bright green and fresh, were draped at the windows. A Matthijs Maris painting hung on the wall behind Philip's desk, and two good reproduction paintings hung on the wall between the two windows. Philip was delighted with his revamped office and was grateful to Barbara for her assistance.

Young David was almost eighteen months now, and was about to experience his first real Christmas. The previous one he had been a baby. Now he was a toddler and apt to get up to all sorts of mischief, when he could escape the watchful eyes of his parents. As Barbara rummaged in the attic for the box of Christmas decorations, she wondered about Philip's happiness in his new position. He sometimes came home late. He usually phoned to say that he had a client coming to see him and would be delayed.

Their social life had changed considerably too. They were invited to dine with the senior partners and various clients. Barbara was beginning to make friends with a number of wives. Occasionally she and Helen Peterson would meet for coffee, or arrange to play badminton in the evenings when their husbands went to their club. Barbara was fortunate in acquiring Ena West, a young girl who lived nearby, to act as babysitter. She could see Philip was enjoying his job, but she felt that at times he seemed a bit pompous. The spontaneity she remembered when they first met had been toned down. It was as if he was putting on an act in front of people.

Christmas that year was a joyous occasion. David was now old enough to enjoy unwrapping his own presents. His little face was a picture as he tore all the wrapping paper into shreds in his eagerness to get to the toys. Philip's parents stayed for a few days, rejoicing in being able to spoil their grandson. Their present was an enormous Teddy Bear, almost as big as the child. He adored it and dragged it around with him everywhere. Harriet came over for Christmas day. She did not seem her usual cheerful and bossy self, and Barbara was worried about her driving back to Stickleburn.

"Are you taking care of yourself Aunt Harriet?" she asked, "You look tired. Please, I wish you'd stay the night with us."

"No Barbara, dear," her great-aunt replied, "I'm going home now. I must admit that I'm feeling a bit tired. I've not been sleeping all that well recently. But I'm all right. I'm a tough old girl. Thanks for a lovely day. That young scamp keeps you busy, but he's adorable. Bless you darling."

Philip had noticed that Harriet avoided him as much as she could, and was worried about it. He wondered if she'd learned that Barbara had financed his partnership, and hoped she wouldn't upset Barbara. "Aunt Harriet didn't seem her usual bright self today did she?" he said to Barbara, as they shut the front door after she left. "I hope she's all right."

"I think she's beginning to feel her age. But she hates us fussing. I'll pop over some day next week. Now I must go and put David to bed. Would you like to be a dear and clear the dining room table. I'll just make some sandwiches for supper. See what your parents would like, please, and pour them both a drink."

Her mother-in-law climbed the stairs slowly in front of Barbara that night. They had left the men downstairs having a nightcap. "My dear," she said to her daughter-in-law, "I think you've done wonders for Philip. He looks so happy and contented. And young David is a joy. Mind you he's at that age when he could be a handful. But I notice you stand no nonsense from him. Thanks for a lovely day. Goodnight, dear." She kissed Barbara on the cheek.

Barbara was relieved to get to bed and sink down onto the pillows. She hoped Philip and his father would not stay too long downstairs. She was almost asleep when she felt her husband slip into bed and his arm coming round her, and she turned so that he enfolded her. She was lovely and warm and receptive to his lovemaking.

"A perfect ending to a perfect day my love" he whispered.

Chapter 21

Towards the end of February the following year, Barbara suspected that she was pregnant again. She decided not to say anything until she had had it confirmed by her doctor. A few days later, Philip woke to find his wife missing from their room and sounds of retching coming from the bathroom. He got up quickly and knocked on the door.

"Are you all right, Barbara?"

A white-faced Barbara opened the door. "No" she snapped, "I'm not all right. I'm pregnant again. I was going to tell you tonight after I've been to see Doctor Reid."

"You don't sound too pleased about it," said Philip.

"Neither would you be if you'd been sick every morning these last few weeks. Sorry Philip. It'll be all right once this month is over."

"When is it due?" asked Philip.

"About the end of September, I suppose. I'll know more tonight."

Philip put his arms round his wife and kissed her forehead. The nauseous smell of her breath was very noticeable.

"Please, I must clean my teeth," she said, and turned from him to go back into the bathroom. Loud noises came from young David's room.

"Please could you pick him up while I wash and get dressed?" she called, "I'll go and get your breakfast ready. I can dress him after he's had his breakfast."

She hurriedly dressed and went down to the sunny kitchen. She opened the back door to let the cat out before filling the kettle. She started to prepare Philip's breakfast. About fifteen minutes later he appeared with David already dressed. Barbara laughed at the sight of the immaculate man with a rather tousle-haired toddler wearing a green jumper over a pair of yellow dungarees. She felt a lot happier. "Thank you darling. That's a great help."

Taking the child from his father's arms she deposited him in his highchair. "Come on young man. Your breakfast is ready too."

She sat down to have a cup of tea and a piece of dry toast while she spooned cereal into David's mouth. He attempted to grab the spoon, which slipped from Barbara's fingers, and then he deposited the bowl of cereal onto the floor while she bent to retrieve the spoon. Philip smiled as Barbara emerged from under the breakfast table. She glared at him and then dissolved into laughter. David's face was a picture as he observed his parents. He had obviously been a bit apprehensive about being scolded for being naughty. Now all three were laughing and happy.

"Barbara," said Philip, "I think that with another baby on the way, we must get another car. You'll need transportation, and I need the car most days. Things are picking up at work and I'm hoping to expand quite a bit. I'll ask around, and see if I can get a small second-hand car for you."

"Don't do anything in a hurry. But with Aunt Harriet's birthday in May, I may have to go over to Porlock more. I've got the invitations and made arrangements with the hotel for the party. I've told her we'll pick her up and take her out for a meal that day. I only hope she doesn't suspect. But she's a shrewd woman, and I can only hope her friends will keep the secret."

Philip finished his breakfast and rose from the table. He kissed his wife and son. As he went towards the door he asked, "When's your appointment this afternoon?"

"Two-thirty. I've got Ena coming to look after David for an hour."

Ena's mother came in twice a week to help Barbara with the housework. Ena babysat for them occasionally. She was going to secretarial college after taking her exams, and was saving the money she made from babysitting to help with her expenses. She was a pretty girl who was ambitious and wished to be independent.

After Philip left, Barbara decided she would take David shopping, once she had cleared the breakfast table. The phone rang just as she was about to leave the house.

"Barbara. It's Helen here. Are you going into town?"

"Well, I'm going to do some shopping with David."

"Care to come and have coffee with me on the way back. There's something I want to discuss with you. Can you make it about eleven?"

"Yes I suppose so. What's it all about?"

"Don't sound so enthusiastic. I'll tell you all about it when I see you. Goodbye."

Barbara replaced the receiver and decided to change out of her slacks into a grey skirt and blue blouse. She picked a navy jacket from her wardrobe, and looked at herself in the mirror. She noticed that she'd recovered her normal colour, instead of the pallid drawn face she'd had earlier. The walk to the shops pushing David did a lot to restore her morale. She really had been fed up this morning, but the spring sunshine made her feel better. She noticed that the trees were breaking into leaf and the daffodils and tulips in the gardens were already in bud. David smiled at people from his pushchair. He was a happy child and Barbara adored him. She just hoped the new baby would be as good.

She made her way towards Helen Peterson's house. They lived two streets behind the Sharps. On arrival, David asked to be let out of his pushchair. Helen employed an au pair to look after her two children. Her older daughter was at school, and Sophie was two. The children were taken to the playroom, and the mothers settled down to have coffee together.

"I asked you over," Helen began, "because George Mead is retiring at the end of May, and we've decided, or rather the partners have decided, to have a party and presentation for him. Ivan Jones is a widower, so it's up to us to arrange the food and drink. I must say I like Ivan. Did you ever meet his wife?"

"No, I didn't. She died five years ago didn't she?"

"Yes. She was a mousy little woman, but Ivan loved her. She died after a hysterectomy that went wrong, and he's been lost without her. I've tried comforting him, but he's a morose man. Didn't get anywhere with him." She smiled to herself, leaving Barbara wondering what she meant.

"Will you help me with the arrangements, Barbara? I know you're arranging your great-aunt's party, and I thought I could call on your expertise."

"I don't know about expertise, Helen. But I'll gladly help. Where are we holding this party?"

For the next hour, the two young women chatted and made plans until it was time Barbara took David home for lunch. As she walked home, she thought about Helen, who was a tall, thin, attractive blonde, in her early thirties. She had a low-pitched sexy voice and enjoyed flirting with men, which annoyed Samuel, her husband. Although Barbara liked Helen as a friend, she wasn't quite sure that she could be trusted. She loved to gossip. So Barbara hadn't wished to tell her about the pregnancy.

When Philip returned home that evening, he was delighted to learn that the pregnancy had been confirmed. On being told about Barbara's meeting with Helen he was even more pleased. "You will help her all you can won't you? With your great-aunt's connections in Taunton, it'll all help with the expansion of the firm, once George retires. Helen is excellent at chatting people up. She's really an asset to Samuel." He paused for a minute before saying as an afterthought, "Just as you are to me, my darling."

He left the room to go up to say "Goodnight" to his son, leaving Barbara, for some reason feeling uneasy when she thought over what Philip had said. Finally she decided that she was just being fanciful.

Chapter 22

In early June, Barbara was ironing in the kitchen when she suddenly cried out in pain. Luckily Mrs West was in the house. She hurried into the kitchen to find Barbara doubled up, holding her stomach.

"Oh no. Please sit down, Mrs Sharp. I'll phone your doctor."

"No, Mrs West. Can you help me upstairs? I think I'll lie down for a little while. It may be cramp." However, another sharp pain made Barbara cry out. It was obvious that all was not well, and Mrs West insisted on phoning for the doctor.

Luckily Doctor Reid had just finished his morning surgery and said he would call straight away. After he had examined Barbara, he said he wanted her to go into hospital for a few day's observation, as there was a possibility of a miscarriage. He phoned Philip, who rather grudgingly said he'd come home and take Barbara into hospital.

Mrs West said she would pack a case to take into the hospital. "Don't you worry, my dear. I'll look after David, with Ena's help. He loves Ena and he'll be no trouble. Just rest for a few days. You've been so busy lately. What with your great-aunt's party and then Mr Meade's farewell do. You've been rushing round like a scalded cat. You've just overdone things. Now you must rest."

Once in the hospital, Barbara was glad when the gynaecologist had finished examining her.

"We'll have to keep you in for a week or two," the consultant concluded, "Just as a precaution. I think the baby is alright, but we've got to make sure that you rest. And you can't do that at home, now can she, Mr Sharp?"

Philip's face fell as he realised the implications. He would have to be responsible for looking after David, or for making arrangements for someone to do it. "I suppose so," he said, "Could she not rest at home with a resident nurse?"

"No. She needs complete peace and rest, and with a small child in the house, she certainly wouldn't get that. I'm afraid her blood pressure is high at present. There is a risk of toxaemia, which could cause her to lose the baby."

Barbara was relieved when they both left the room. She sobbed once the door was closed. A little while later a nurse entered with some pills for her to swallow, and shortly afterwards she fell asleep..

Philip drove home, annoyed that he might have to take some time off work. He had some very important clients he was trying to impress.

Mrs West had waited until his return. She could understand his dilemma. "Look, Mr Sharp. Ena and I can look after David for you. I'll take him home with me, and then you won't have to worry about him. He knows us. And I'll come in as usual twice a week. In fact I can prepare a meal for you each day, so that all you'll have to do is heat it up when you come home. You can manage breakfast yourself."

"Yes, Mrs West, thanks. But don't bother about the meal. I can cook a little myself, or eat at a restaurant in town. I'll manage. Oh, by the way, which days do you come in?"

"Tuesdays and Fridays."

They agreed on a sum for looking after David. "That will be fine Mrs West." said Philip, "Thanks for offering to have him. It eases my mind to know he's with someone we know and trust. I'll give you a lift home when you're ready."

"I'm ready now. I've packed a case with clothes for David. I'd be grateful for a lift. Oh, we'd better take his pushchair too. Ena can take him for walks in the park. We've a cot at home – it's the one we had for our family and it comes in handy when our grandchildren come to stay. Give my regards to Mrs Sharp when you visit her later. Tell her not to worry over the little lad."

On his return home in the evening, having visited Barbara in hospital, he sank gratefully into his chair with a large glass of whisky in his hand. His thoughts were in turmoil, as he'd spoken to the gynaecologist again, who was worried about Barbara's condition. She was exhausted, and her high blood pressure was a cause for concern. They would have to keep a close eye on her for the rest of the pregnancy.

Philip's thought ran on the lines of the worst scenario. If she died he would not inherit the house. It would be David's, but her inheritance would surely be his. He tried to push the thought from his mind. There was no doubt he loved his wife dearly. He knew he was being selfish and eager to obtain more capital for his own ends. But his ambition seemed to drive him on. He knew that he must try and be patient, and be more understanding and loving towards Barbara.

Philip took David in to visit his mother only once, with disastrous consequences. The child screamed and cried hysterically when he was told to kiss his mother goodbye. His cries echoed in Barbara's ears as Philip hurriedly carried him out of the ward. It was decided he wouldn't visit again.

"It's too upsetting for him, darling," said Philip, "The doctors think it would be better for all concerned – the staff, patients as well as you."

"I miss you both so much," cried Barbara, "I just long to be home."

She was in hospital for four weeks in June, and was only allowed home on condition that she rested.

Aunt Harriet had been determined there should be someone in the house to cope with David on Barbara's return. She talked it over with Philip, and they had agreed that Ena West should live in until the baby's birth. She was only too happy to do so, as it gave her a chance to earn some more money for when she started college in the autumn.

By September Barbara was becoming so weary. The gynaecologist was adamant that she needed to be quiet, or she could lose the baby. She was relieved to relax. She'd suffered from nausea for most of the first five months, and at least in hospital she'd have a chance to regain her strength.

During the last two months of her pregnancy, Philip made excuses about having to work late and was inclined to be offhand with both David and Barbara. On several occasions he'd come home smelling strongly of alcohol, and had been sharp when Barbara commented on it. "Good God! Can't I have a drink or two with friends without you complaining? You're not much company at present are you? It's not much fun having a wife who looks like a pregnant cow."

Barbara was extremely hurt and angered by his remark. "Well it's as much your fault as it is mine. It took both of us to make this child. You not only smell of whisky, but there's lipstick on your cheek. I presume your friends are not all male?"

His face flushed and he guiltily looked in the mirror in the hall to see where the offending lipstick was. "Helen and her friend Marcia Penhalligon were at the club, and they kissed me as I left," he explained.

Barbara was suspicious, and inclined to query the excuse. However, she decided they were both tired and stressed.

Anne Louise Sharp was born in the first week of September, weighing in at seven pounds, five ounces. She had an excellent pair of lungs from the moment of her birth, and was a greedy babe. It had been a relatively easy birth, and Barbara was glad to discover she'd once again regained her figure very quickly.

On returning from the hospital, Barbara decided that until Anne slept through the night, she would sleep in the spare room, so that Philip would have undisturbed sleep. When, after six weeks, the baby was settled into a routine, Barbara moved back into their own bedroom. Philip had made no overtures towards making love to her during that time. He said that he was heeding Dr Reid's warnings that she needed time to recover from the pregnancy.

That night she planned a celebratory meal. The table was set beautifully, and the flickering light from two candles was reflected in the shining surface of the lovely polished table. Barbara had gone to great lengths to make herself attractive. She'd had her hair cut and shampooed into a more sophisticated style, and bought herself a new soft blue wool dress, which showed off her slim figure to perfection. She had settled the children, and eagerly awaited Philip's return from the office.

When six-thirty came with no sign of her husband's arrival, she began to worry. She phoned the office, but there was no reply. By seven-thirty she was really anxious and decided to phone his club. The secretary hesitated slightly when she asked if her husband was there. Eventually he said. "I don't think that I've seen him tonight. Mr Peterson and Mr Jones are here though. Do you want to speak to one of them? They may know where he is."

Suddenly Barbara heard the car being driven into the garage.

"Thank you, John. He's just arrived. So it's all right."

When Philip entered the hall he saw his wife replacing the telephone receiver. "Who was that on the phone?" he asked.

"I was checking the club to see if you were there, as you were late. I'd planned a special meal for us, darling."

"I was working at the office," he replied in a cool voice.

"I'd already phoned there, and there was no reply."

He shrugged his shoulders and quietly said "I decided not to answer the phone as I didn't want to be disturbed. I'd got some accounts that needed extra work before I gave them to my client. Anyway, why are we having a special meal?"

"Because, my love, I've moved back into our bedroom. Anne is sleeping through the night and I miss you beside me."

Philip turned from hanging his coat in the cupboard and smiled sheepishly at her. "That is a cause for celebration. How about a drink before supper?"

"There's a bottle of bubbly in the fridge. It's one of the ones Aunt Harriet gave us. Would you like to open it while I put the vegetables on to boil?"

Philip moved swiftly to sweep his wife into his arms and kissed her passionately. Desire ran through Barbara as she felt his hard body against hers. Eventually they made their way towards the kitchen and while Philip opened the champagne, he noticed how attractive his wife looked. A guilty feeling ran through him, as he knew that he had been neglecting her for months. She had been generous in helping him to acquire the partnership, and he should have been more grateful and considerate towards her.

"You're looking very beautiful tonight, my love," he murmured, "That dress is a knockout. I've not seen it before have I? I shall have to watch out the next time we go to the club together. You'll have all the men round you like bees round a honey pot. I do love you so much."

Barbara gave a sigh of happiness as he kissed her again. With a possessive arm round her waist he steered her into the study, where he proceeded to pour out the champagne.

"I propose a toast to my gorgeous wife and two wonderful children. You've given me so much and made me so happy."

"Here's to all of us," replied Barbara. Her eyes shone brightly as she smiled at her husband.

Chapter 23

During the next year the Sharps seemed to be the epitome of a model family. At least Barbara thought they were. Young David went to play school in the mornings, and Barbara made friends with other mothers and became involved in a number of activities at the school. Anne had grown into a chubby fair-haired toddler who, like her brother at that age, was mischievous.

Aunt Harriet, now in her seventies, had slowed down considerably. She no longer judged flower shows or gave talks, but she loved her garden. Her cottage at Stickleburn was maintained with the help of Dick and May Passmore. Dick did all the heavy digging work in the garden, and May helped in the house. They all looked forward to the visits Barbara made with the children.

Occasionally during these visits she saw Michael Burgess, and obtained news of Bill Franks, who, after his short service commission in the Navy, had trained as an orthopaedic surgeon. He was living in Bristol now with his wife Beth, who'd been a nursing sister at the Naval Hospital in Plymouth. Michael also told Barbara that he was seeing a lot of Jane Hart, who was now working as a solicitor in Bristol.

"I'm rather hoping we'll get engaged soon," he went on, "She has a good practice, and I'm not sure if she's ready to give it up to become a farmer's wife. I've been lucky in having some success as a breeder of race horses too. Mother and Father are keen to retire, and want me to take over the running of the farm. They intend building a bungalow in a corner of the meadow, and have just got planning permission. If I take on the farm now, it should save death duties later on. That sounds awful doesn't it? But so many farms and estates are being crippled by inheritance tax. Father asked Jane about it a few months ago, when she was down for the weekend. She agreed and gave us some advice."

Barbara was delighted at the thought that her two old friends were contemplating getting married. She'd seen little of Jane in the last few years, and realised how much she'd missed her. Jane had been such an important part of her life when her parents had been killed.

"Michael, that is wonderful news. I wish you both all the best. Jane has kept this very quiet, hasn't she? I expect it's my fault really, because with the children to cope with, I've been kept pretty busy. I'm afraid I've not been in touch as much as I should. She's always been such a good friend to me."

"I'm hoping she'll be down this weekend," said Michael, "Perhaps we may have some news later."

"That would be wonderful. Look, how about coming over for a meal with us on Saturday evening? It's such ages since I've seen Jane, and we'd love you to come. Seven thirty?"

"I'd love to, Barbara. Can I let you know tomorrow? I'll be phoning Jane tonight, and I'll see what she says. But I'm sure she'll be pleased to see you."

Barbara drove back to Taunton that evening, hoping that Jane and Michael would get engaged. They'd been firm friends to her for over ten years.

Michael phoned the next day to say he and Jane would love to come over on Saturday evening. Barbara was delighted, and planned her menu carefully. She knew that Jane had not really approved of Philip, and thought that was possibly the reason she'd not seen so much of her old friend. Barbara also suspected that Philip was slightly wary of Jane, but she couldn't understand why. When she had told him her friends were coming over for dinner on the Saturday, he'd not seemed terribly interested.

"Oh all right. If that's what you want. Haven't seen Michael for ages. I gather his horses are doing well. May get some tips for the next race," was all he said.

Barbara was putting the finishing touches to the dining table, when she heard Michael's sports car pull up outside. She called to Philip in the study, "They're here, darling. Let's see if we need the champagne."

"Jane, how great it is to see you." Barbara cried, as her friend came to the door. "You look stunning. Very much the successful business woman."

They hugged each other while the men greeted each other.

"Haven't seen you around for some time, Philip," said Michael.

"Well, business keeps me tied to the office, I'm afraid, and what spare time I have, I spend with Barbara and the children. I don't get across to Porlock very often these days. Let's go and have a drink before the girls come through."

Barbara turned quickly round at that remark, and holding Jane's left hand up she smiled broadly and said, "We'll have the champagne that's in the fridge. So go and get it darling. We have something to celebrate. Isn't it wonderful? Two of my best friends are engaged. Bless you both. The ring is lovely."

Jane's face was radiant as Barbara admired the diamond and emerald ring.

"Congratulations Michael," she added, "I hope you'll both be very happy. Have you decided when the wedding will be and where?"

"Hold your horses, Barbara" Michael laughed, with his arms round both young women. "We've not decided yet. We haven't had a chance to discuss it properly. But we'll probably wait until the bungalow is built for my parents. It should be finished next April or May."

Philip arrived with the tray of glasses, and made a rather pompous speech before proposing the couple's health. Barbara gave him a puzzled look. Why was he acting so strangely? She knew he could be pompous at times, but why tonight? She mentally shrugged the thought out of her mind, and the conversation about the wedding plans took over.

When the guests had left later, Philip was very thoughtful and quiet. As he lay in bed waiting for Barbara to join him he said. "I can't remember which firm Jane is with in Bristol, can you? She should be able to get a job with one of the practices in Minehead, if she still wants to work. Though I expect she'll find plenty to do on the farm. Michael has improved and modernised things there. He seems to be a very successful horse breeder."

Barbara and Jane had spent time together in the kitchen after dinner. They had discussed what had happened to themselves over the years since Barbara's wedding. It had been an opportunity to catch up on all the gossip. Jane had queried Barbara about how Philip was enjoying being with the firm of Mead, Jones and Peterson. It was as if she was anxious that all was well. She'd been happy to be reassured by Barbara, and had then dropped the subject.

Now, as Barbara brushed her hair, she thought about the conversation. It had been odd of Jane to question how things were. It was really none of her business. "Philip," she asked her husband, "Is everything all right with the firm?"

He looked at his wife's face in the dressing table mirror with a startled expression. "Why do you ask that?" he asked.

"Well, Jane asked me that question earlier this evening, and I just wondered why."

"Everything's fine. Jane is just a suspicious lawyer. I'm tired. Come on to bed. The children will be awake soon."

For the next few months life continued smoothly, although Philip was often late home. During the summer, the family had gone to Devon for two weeks and the children enjoyed playing on the beach at Hope Cove. They had taken a cottage, and Ena West, on vacation from her Secretarial Course, had accompanied them to help look after David and Anne. Ena had really blossomed since going to college, and her mother was very proud of her. She was due to start work in September. She was trustworthy and reliable, which allowed Barbara to relax. Most evenings Philip took his wife out to dinner in one of the local hotels.

For Barbara, this was two weeks of peace. She loved the quiet tranquillity of the little village. It was completely unspoilt, and the children were happy playing and splashing about in the water under Ena's eagle eye. Philip had taken up golf, and went nearly every morning to Thurlstone, where he could be sure of getting a partner to accompany him on a round.

Sitting on the beach, Barbara watched her two children as they played. David was growing up to be a sturdy youngster. His brown hair was becoming streaked with the sun. When he looked up at his mother, a wide mischievous grin would light up his face. Anne was beginning to lose her baby chubbiness, and she wanted to follow her big brother everywhere. This sometimes led to screams and tantrums.

Years later, Barbara realised that this was really the happiest time with Philip and the children. She had the joy of watching their children happy and safe in the love and attention of their parents. She had no inkling that her life was to be disturbed in the near future.

Chapter 24

Shortly after their return home, Barbara received a phone call from May Passmore telling her that her great-aunt had fallen and broken her leg. She'd been rushed to hospital in Taunton. Mrs West was hurriedly called in to look after the children, while Barbara drove to the hospital.

She was in time to see Harriet before she was taken down to theatre to have her leg set. Her great-aunt's face was grey and drawn with pain, but her indomitable spirit shone through. She managed to assure her niece that all would be well.

"Guess who's going to operate on me?" she said with a wry smile.

"I don't care who operates on you, as long as they do a good job of it," answered Barbara.

"Bill Franks is now the orthopaedic surgeon in charge, so I have no qualms at all. I'll be back on my feet in no time."

"I'm staying until you are back in the ward," said Barbara, as she kissed her great-aunt before she was wheeled down the corridor. Barbara then went to sit in the waiting room.

Two hours later, Bill Franks appeared at the door, and smiling gently at her, told her the operation had been a success. "The only thing I'm worried about is that your great-aunt is such an independent woman. It will take her some time to adjust to the fact that she won't be able to do as much as she would like. It was a nasty fracture, and because of her age she'll have to take extra care. Do you think she'll obey our orders?"

"I doubt it very much, Bill, but I'll certainly keep an eye on her. I'm glad it was you who operated on her. She has great faith in you."

"Well we have known each other for quite a long time, and

I've always had a great admiration for her. It is nice to see you again, Barbara."

"We must get together soon Bill. I'd love to meet your wife. Perhaps you could come and meet my family."

"I'd like that Barbara. We're in the process of buying a house on the outskirts of Norton Fitzwarren. Beth is looking forward to having a permanent home at last. I'd like you to meet her. I hear you have two delightful children."

"According to Aunt Harriet, I suppose. They're always good with her. She has a knack of being able to keep them under control just with a look, which is more than I'm able to do. Have you any children, Bill?"

"Not yet, but we keep hoping. I must go and see to my patients. I think your great-aunt should be out of recovery, and back into the ward. Just take great care of her. She's a wonderful old girl. Hope to see you soon."

Barbara walked along to the ward. She was very pleased that she'd seen Bill again, and felt a little envious of his wife. She remembered how much she'd liked him when she'd been a teenager. And he had become a very handsome man. Distinguished looking, with a confident air about him.

Harriet was very drowsy when Barbara sat down at her bedside. She asked for some things to be brought from her home. Barbara promised she would go straight out to Stickleburn to collect them. She managed to phone and let Mrs West know, and asked her if she could feed the children and put them to bed, and let her husband know what had happened.

"Mr Sharp phoned earlier to say that he'd be late home," reported Mrs West. He had to go to a meeting in Bristol. But don't you worry. I'll stay on until you come back. The children are fine. Your great-aunt needs you at present."

Driving to her great-aunt's house, she began to worry about what would happen if Aunt Harriet should die. She'd been so much a part of Barbara's life for so long. She realised that despite losing her parents when she was sixteen, she'd been fortunate in having such a loving and caring person to act as her guardian. She couldn't imagine life without her. She had to tell herself not to be so morbid. Her great-aunt wasn't going to die. She was a tough old woman and at any rate Barbara needed her.

Arriving at the cottage, May Passmore helped her to collect nightdresses and toiletries, and pack them into a case. Barbara reassured May that her great-aunt was in good hands, and asked her to continue to look after the cottage. Then she drove back to the hospital, where she found that her great-aunt was awake and had been able to drink a cup of tea. She left the hospital feeling calmer about Harriet's condition.

When she got home she found that the children were already in bed. "Thank you very much Mrs West. I really am so grateful to you for looking after the children. My great-aunt is much more comfortable now, but I'll have to make sure she behaves herself when she's allowed home."

"If there's anything I can do to help, just ask," replied Mrs West, "I know she has May Passmore to help in the house. It might be a good idea to have a bed downstairs for her, as her leg will still be in plaster, won't it?"

"That is a good idea. I'll put it to her when she's feeling stronger. She won't be allowed out until she can walk with crutches, will she? She'll probably hate that, and will be all grouchy and cross. Oh well, we've had enough excitement for one day. Did my husband say when he'd be back when he phoned?"

"He said he'd be late and not to wait up for him. There was quite a lot of noise in the background when he phoned. I think he was already in Bristol."

"Funny, he didn't mention anything about a meeting this morning. He's had quite a few to go to lately."

"Hmm," said Mrs West. "Well, I'd better get off or my old man will think I've run off with the baker."

"That would never do would it?" Barbara smiled at Mrs West, as she was putting on her coat. "Thanks again. I don't know what I'd do without you."

Once the door was closed she went up to look at David and Anne. Both were sound asleep. With a sigh of relief, she went downstairs and poured herself a glass of sherry. She was tired, and wished that Philip hadn't had to go to Bristol. She could have done with cuddling up beside him on the settee and telling him about her great-aunt and her meeting with Bill Franks again.

In her mind she went over the day's happenings, and she remembered Mrs West's remarks as she was leaving. Suddenly that "Hmm" she had uttered gave Barbara a frisson of suspicion. It was as if Mrs West knew something, but wasn't prepared to divulge what it was. Barbara thought too that she had felt there were rather a lot of trips to Bristol recently, and that Philip had been evasive about the reasons. On three occasions he had stayed overnight but hadn't mentioned at which hotel. He had been really quite short with her when she had questioned him.

"No, he wouldn't, would he?" she asked herself aloud.

But the thoughts didn't leave her. There were a lot of things that needed explaining. He had too much to lose if he had been playing around, but something had definitely been missing from their marriage in the past few months. He had also mentioned that there were some areas in the firm that needed tightening up.

At eleven o'clock, feeling depressed and exhausted by the events of the day Barbara decided to go to bed.

Chapter 25

At two o'clock she awoke suddenly, as she heard car tyres skidding on the drive. The car door slammed, and she turned on the bedside light as she heard a loud curse. There was a clatter and more cursing. Putting on her dressing gown, she went downstairs and, on opening the front door, she saw her husband slowly getting to his feet. He had obviously stumbled up the steps, and appeared to be very drunk.

"Philip, what sort of state are you in? Have you driven from Bristol like this? You must be mad to have driven in that condition. What on earth possessed you?"

"Stop nagging, woman!" he shouted at her. "I'm back safe and sound. What more do you want?"

"I think I'm entitled to an explanation of why you're so late and so drunk. I've been worried enough about Aunt Harriet, without having to worry about you as well. It's not like you to be so inconsiderate."

Philip staggered into the study, while Barbara locked the front door. Following him, she found him about to pour himself a whisky.

"Don't you think you've had enough tonight? It's time you were in bed."

"Always the precious Aunt Harriet. I get fed up with the old bitch. Stop nagging."

Barbara was furious with him and her eyes blazed with fury. "How dare you insult my great-aunt. She's in hospital with a broken leg, and I've been very worried about her. You, on the other hand, seem to have been quite oblivious to what's been happening at home."

He turned to face her and saw just how angry she was. She could see that he was now ill at ease. In a wheedling tone of voice he said. "Babs, I need some money, and I need it soon.

You've got to give it to me." His voice was slurred and he sounded desperate.

"Why should I?" asked Barbara coolly, "You said the business was doing well."

"I need a few thousand to pay off some debts I've incurred. I borrowed some money from a client's account to invest, and the company hasn't done as well as I'd hoped. If I don't pay it back I could be convicted of fraud. You've got to get me out of this mess."

"Why should I? I've already paid for your share in the firm. That money is mine. What about your own savings? Don't tell me that you've lost those too?"

Philip's attitude changed and he strode across the room to shut the door before turning round. With staring eyes, he lifted his left arm and swiped Barbara across the face. As she fell, she hit her head against the edge of the bookcase, knocking herself unconscious for a moment or two. When she came to, she was aware that Philip was on top of her, raping her harshly. As he thrust himself into her he was calling her a selfish bitch who'd led a sheltered life and had no idea of his needs. "I've had better lays with the tarts of Bristol than with you," he shouted, "You're an innocent in trying to please a man. Some of your so-called friends are better in bed than you. I need that money. You'd better get it for me, or you'll suffer." As he came to a climax, he collapsed on her. He had passed out. The amount of drink he had consumed had overcome him.

Somehow she managed to wriggle herself out from under his dead weight. She left him on the floor as she fled upstairs, where she locked herself into the bedroom. Shuddering with shock and pain, she ran herself a hot bath. She felt unclean. Her head throbbed, and there was a deep cut above her right eye, which was bleeding profusely. She lay immersed in the hot water, to which she had added Dettol, and sobbed her heart out. Eventually she let the water out of the bath and dried herself. Putting on a clean nightdress, she clambered into bed. She lay wondering what she had done to deserve this treatment from Philip, and how changed he had become from the polite, charming man she had first met. Her earlier suspicions had been confirmed. He had been unfaithful to her.

She must have dozed off. She was wakened about six-thirty to hear Philip knocking gently on the door. "Barbara, please let me in. I'm sorry about last night. Please open the door and let me apologise. I was too drunk to understand what I was doing or saying. Barbara, please."

"Go into the guest room while I get dressed, and then I'll talk to you. Don't disturb the children, and don't you dare lay a finger on me again."

Getting out of bed she felt dizzy and nauseous. Looking at herself in the mirror, she saw that her right eye was almost closed, and the cut above was red and angry looking. Furious with Philip, she got dressed quickly. She unlocked the door. Entering the guest room, she flung a suit shirt and clean underwear on to a chair. Looking at Philip with anger and disdain, she told him, "When you've cleaned yourself up and got dressed, we'll talk in the study. I have nothing to say to you until then."

"Darling I am so sorry. I love you."

"Did you hear what I said? I'll talk to you in the study later," she said, through gritted teeth.

Philip realised that his gentle wife had a heart of steel that he'd never envisaged. How was he going to deal with her? Looking at her face, he knew that he'd made a big mistake in hitting her. But he was desperate. He knew that if she didn't help him financially he was in deep trouble. He had misused ten thousand pounds of client's money, and now he had to account for it. He was frightened of the consequences, and knew that he'd jeopardised his marriage as well. His thoughts as he hurriedly changed into clean clothes were in turmoil. How could he talk his way out of this situation? He had only a vague idea of what had occurred early this morning, and he had a throbbing headache. Swallowing a couple of aspirin, he made his way to the study, which was empty.

Barbara had been busy in the kitchen. He cautiously opened the kitchen door, to be told firmly that she would bring strong black coffee to the study when she was ready. This was a Barbara that he'd never seen before. He knew by the tone of her voice that she was not in the mood for any excuse from him. He only hoped that he could make her understand it had all been a terrible mistake, and that he really loved her. He was shattered by his behaviour. It had threatened all his hopes and ambitions. He knew he had to act repentant, and beg for forgiveness. He could lose everything.

Standing looking out of the window, he turned as Barbara entered the room with a tray. She placed it on the coffee table. Closing the door she said, "Sit down and drink your coffee."

He did as he was told. She sat down opposite him.

He noticed how badly hurt her head was. "Darling, I am so sorry for hitting out at you. I'm in trouble financially, and I need your help. I promise this will be the last time I will ever ask you for money. I'll pay you back somehow."

"Yes, you will," she answered, "And with interest. I sincerely hope you will never find an occasion to hit me again. Your behaviour this morning was unforgivable. You raped me. You disgust me. I thought we had a happy marriage, but I've been deluding myself for ages. You've admitted that you've been unfaithful to me. I wonder which of my so-called friends have accommodated you? Your late nights and trips to Bristol have all been a cover up for your flings. Well, they're welcome to you."

Philip tried to interrupt, but she held up her hand. "Shut up and listen to me. This is what I've decided. I'll help you pay your debts this time. But we'll have a properly signed agreement, and you will pay me back as and when you can. So much every month into a special account, in trust for the children. I'm not having their inheritance frittered away by their father. I'll get Jane Hart to draw up a contract."

"Please, not an official contract. I don't want it known locally what I've done. I'm so ashamed."

"Oh, please be quiet. I'm not finished with you yet. I can trust Jane's discretion. She'll keep quiet for my sake. How much of your own savings have you got left, and how much do you owe?"

"I owe ten thousand, and I've only got six thousand left."

"God, what a fool you are. So, you'll pay five thousand, and I'll lend you five thousand. But, if you ever do anything like this again, I promise I'll divorce you. As it is, in future you'll sleep in the guest room. I do not want you in my bed at present. I feel unclean after your performance this morning. Do not think you can soft soap me this time. I've got the measure of you at last. I may only have one good eye at present, but believe me, my mind has certainly been sharpened. As far as the children are concerned, we'll try and act naturally in front of them, and with friends and relations. We'll put a good face on it, but I warn you, if you ever behave in that manner again, you'll be out on your ear. Oh, and for the record, I tripped and hit my head on the bookcase. I don't want people speculating about my injury. Now you can get your own breakfast if you feel you can stomach it."

With that she got up and walked out of the room, leaving him stunned by what she had said. This was a Barbara he did not recognise and he was taken aback. He knew that he had really landed himself in a terrible situation.

Chapter 26

Barbara got David and Anne ready for school. They'd both been upset when they saw their mother's face. She explained that she'd hit her head on the bookcase. It throbbed and ached as she drove the children to school, and she could hardly see out of her right eye. On her return, she phoned Jane at her office in Bristol and asked if she could arrange a meeting with her as soon as possible. "I can't explain on the phone, Jane," she said, "But I want your advice professionally."

"All very mysterious. Can you come up to Bristol tomorrow, and we can have lunch together? Then you can tell me what all this is about. How's Aunt Harriet? Michael told me last night of her accident."

"I'm going to visit her this afternoon, and hope she'll be feeling better. She was not too bad last night when I left her. I'll tell you all about it when I see you. I'll come to your office about twelve, if that's all right with you?"

"Yes Barbara. You sound different. Are you okay?"

"I'm just a bit tired, and I've had a bit of a shock. Tell you all about it tomorrow. Bye."

She then phoned Helen Peterson, and asked if she could look after Anne this afternoon while she visited her great-aunt. She had phoned the hospital and been told that Harriet had a restful night and was chomping at the bit to get out of bed.

"Sounds as if she's her old self," said Barbara. "Tell her I'll be in this afternoon and she'd better behave herself.'

The sister laughed and said, "I've a feeling we'll probably have to tie her to the bed for a day or two. She's complaining that she can't use a bedpan. Never has and never will. How we're going to get over that hurdle I am not sure. We'll just have to wait and see. She's certainly a bright spark."

Somehow Barbara got through the morning. She felt dizzy at times, and lay down on her bed for an hour, having taken two painkillers. But she couldn't really rest. Everything that had happened recently ran through her brain. She had always been loving and caring towards Philip, and thought they had a happy marriage. Now she felt disillusioned by the events of last night. She'd been madly in love with him, and had wanted no other man. She had felt fulfilled when the children were born. She still cared for him in a way, but knew that she could no longer trust him. At twenty-eight, she had stopped being naïve. She had grown up and matured, and now she would no longer tolerate Philip taking her for granted.

After a light lunch of a cup of Oxo and a dry biscuit, she deposited Anne with Helen, who exclaimed when she saw Barbara's face. "What on earth happened to your face? It looks terrible. Have you seen a doctor? That looks nasty."

Barbara just said that she'd stumbled and hit her head. Helen's eyebrows raised and she said laughingly, "You'd better take more water with it."

"Believe me, I was stone cold sober when I did it. Unlike my dear husband, who came home at two o'clock, drunk as a lord."

Helen noticed the bitterness in Barbara's voice. "Oh had he been out with the boys?" she asked.

"At present I don't care where he'd been. He's not exactly my favourite person. I must go and see Aunt Harriet now. Thanks for looking after Anne. I'll pick her up after I've collected David."

Barbara regretted having let Helen know how she felt.

When she arrived at the hospital ward where Aunt Harriet was, the sister took one look at her face and insisted that it was examined before she went into see her great-aunt. The registrar gently felt the cut and examined her eye. On being told how the injury had occurred he said. "Well, I don't think there's any damage to the eye, but I'd like to put a couple of stitches in that cut. It's a pity you didn't come to Casualty straight away."

He gently stitched the cut and put a dressing on it. "Your great-aunt will probably insist you get into the next bed beside her," he said. "She is much better. We've solved the problem of the bedpan with a commode. But she still hates it. She really is quite a character. Mr Franks has been making her laugh. They obviously know each other well."

"I'm glad he's seen her today. He seems such a good surgeon. We've known him a long time. His cousin is marrying my best friend next year. I'd better go and see my great-aunt. I only hope I don't scare her with this dressing you've put on. I feel like Popeye."

Barbara smiled her thanks at the registrar and the sister, and made her way to her great-aunt's bedside.

"What the hell's happened to you, girl?" exclaimed Harriet. "I'm the one who's been in the wars. Are you trying to steal my thunder? Seriously, my girl, what on earth has happened?"

Barbara told her the story, hoping that it would be believed. Then she hurriedly changed the subject by suggesting that Dick and May Passmore brought a bed downstairs in the cottage for when Harriet returned to Stickleburn. Harriet thought it was an excellent idea, certainly until she got the plaster off. She had become quite reconciled to having to stay in Taunton hospital for a week or so. She asked after the children, and Barbara promised to bring them in on the Saturday afternoon for a quick visit.

"Oh, by the way," she added, "I'm going up to Bristol tomorrow by train to see Jane Hart. So I'll be in to see you in the evening. We're having lunch together. I must go and pick up David and Anne. If there's anything you need, tell the sister to give me a ring. I love you, Aunt Harriet. Bless you."

She kissed her great-aunt and left, feeling that she wanted to cry.

Harriet was left feeling a bit tired, and suspicious that there was something Barbara was keeping from her. The bruising on her face and the cut worried her. Was Barbara telling her the truth about her falling and hurting herself against the bookcase?

In the evening, after playing with the children and getting them to bed early, Barbara decided not to prepare anything for the evening meal. She wasn't hungry, and Philip could get his own meal on his return. She was weary, and her body felt as if every bone ached. Her head still throbbed, but she was determined to face Philip. This was her home, and he was not going to be intimidated by him. Somehow, she had to find the strength to cope.

He arrived home about seven, expecting to be greeted by his children. He was crestfallen to learn that they were both in bed, and that if he wanted anything to eat he could get it. He was also shocked at his wife's appearance with the dressing over her right eye. "What explanation did you give the doctor?" he asked, frightened that she may have given the true version of what had occurred.

"Frightened I may have told the truth? God, you make me sick. No. I told them I'd fallen against the bookcase, and no further explanation. Satisfied? You really are a coward aren't you? I've had enough for one day. Get your own meal. I'm going to bed and my door will be locked. So don't bother to try to get in. The children are asleep. Tomorrow I'm going to Bristol to see Jane, and get her to draw up a contract. I'll give you the cheque for the five thousand on Thursday, and you'd better have your own chequebook ready then too. I want to be with you when you pay it into your client's account. It will be a long time before I trust you again. If ever."

With that she walked out of the room and went upstairs, leaving her husband open mouthed at the change in her. The innocent young girl he had married had somehow discovered that she was made of steel. The transformation left him feeling helpless, and very sorry for himself. But he knew that he had brought it all on himself by his behaviour.

Barbara meanwhile soaked her aching body in a hot bath. She still felt as if she would never be clean again. Once she had dried herself, she swallowed two painkillers and climbed into bed. She knew that she needed a good night's sleep before going to Bristol to see Jane. She only hoped she was doing the right thing, but felt sure Jane would advise her. She thought she had enough evidence to sue Philip for a divorce, but for the sake of the children it was unthinkable. Tomorrow was another day. Surely things couldn't get worse.

Chapter 27

Next morning she left Mrs West. to cope with the children until her return from Bristol. She did some shopping before she went to Jane's office.

"My God," gasped Jane, as they hugged each other, "What on earth has happened to you?"

Barbara dissolved into tears as Jane led her to a seat. Once her friend was settled, Jane went to a cupboard and poured some brandy into a glass. She handed it to Barbara saying, "For medicinal purposes only."

Barbara gulped it down quickly. "Thanks Jane. I needed that before I tell you what happened, and what I want you to do for me." She then proceeded to tell Jane the true story of what had occurred and what she proposed to do.

"I didn't want to go to Mr McGrath," she concluded, "As I don't want Aunt Harriet to know anything about it. They are trustees of the estate, and he would be bound to tell her. Luckily I have savings of my own, so they don't have to know what I'm giving, or rather lending, Philip"

Jane was horrified by the story, but could see that Barbara needed her to act for her in drawing up a legal contract. She suggested that she and Michael call over the weekend at a convenient time and get Philip to sign the document, and they would witness it. She also suggested that she should keep a copy. "I've never really trusted him and I'd like to know that you have a backup copy as well. Don't worry. I won't tell Michael what it's about. I'll just say it's a business transaction, and we won't stay long. I don't think I could be civil to Philip at present."

They had lunch together, and Barbara returned to her home feeling relieved at what she had done. Jane had been very understanding and sympathetic towards her friend.

On the Saturday evening Philip duly signed the contract, with a very sour expression on his face. Jane and Michael made the excuse that they were going back to the farm, so they didn't stay long.

When they left, Philip turned to Barbara saying. "Are you happy now? You've got me over a barrel."

"You put yourself there. No, I am not happy. But at least your children won't have to visit you in jail, and you're out of trouble for the time being."

Two months went by with an icy atmosphere between husband and wife when they were by themselves. In front of the children and friends they put on a united front.

Harriet was now back in her own home, and was managing to get around with the aid of a stick. This last Christmas she had spent alone, as she hadn't felt she could cope with the children and the stairs in Barbara's house. However, they visited her for a short time on Boxing Day. Even in the short time they were there, Harriet had sensed that all was not well between her great-niece and her husband. She saw through the false heartiness of Philip. She decided to put on hold her determination to get to the bottom of what was wrong. She had to get Barbara on her own. Now was not the time.

Barbara looked pale and weary. The scar over her eye still showed clearly. Philip avoided being alone with Harriet, and scarcely looked at her. He was polite and solicitous towards her, but there was no eye contact. Harriet had been reminded of what her first impression had been. Sharp by name and sharp by nature, she recalled.

"Business going well?" she asked Philip politely.

"Bit slow at present, but it'll pick up in the New Year I expect," he answered. "Ivan Jones is thinking of moving back to Wales, so we'll be looking for a new partner. Samuel Peterson thinks he knows of someone. We could do with some new blood. Taunton is growing so fast. We'll need someone who's bright and keen."

Barbara looked across at him. "This is the first I've heard of it. Why haven't you told me?" she asked sharply.

Philip smiled falsely at her. "Well dear. We've both been so busy in our separate ways lately, haven't we? Ivan only told us last week, so we've not gone into it in any depth yet."

Harriet decided to change the subject. "I had a visit from Bill Franks and his wife last week," she said brightly, "They were staying the weekend with the Burgesses. Jane was there too. The new bungalow is certainly coming along nicely. It should be ready for George and Moira to move into by March. The kitchen's going to be very modern, although Moira has insisted on having an Aga cooker. She is so used to one, and says she can't cook on anything else. Michael and Jane are getting married after Easter, you know."

"Yes," said Barbara, "Jane told me. She's so happy. Tell me, what's Bill's wife like? I've never met her. He is as charming as ever and such a good surgeon. Everyone speaks so highly of him."

Harriet answered, "She is rather delicate looking. Dark hair and brown eyes, with a lovely smile. She was a Naval Nursing Sister he met in Plymouth. She doesn't look very strong, but she has a delightful manner. They've moved into their house in Norton Fitzwarren, and she loves it. They seem so happy. No children as yet, but they keep hoping. You must meet them sometime. You'd like her, Barbara."

David and Anne were becoming a bit noisy and bored. They'd spent the time chasing the dog all over the house and garden, and it was clear Harriet was beginning to tire. Barbara washed up the tea dishes and put them away. It was time to take the children away before Harriet became exhausted.

"Come and say goodbye and thank you," she said to them, "Then we must go home."

The children did as they were told and Philip took them out to the car having already made his farewell.

"Come and see me on your own," said Harriet, "Something's bothering you. I know you so well, but I don't want to interfere. Bless you, darling, and thank you for coming."

Barbara's eyes filled with tears as she hugged her great-aunt, and she promised to come over once the children were back at school.

Back in Taunton, she put the children to bed, while Philip sat in the study reading.

He was fed up with the awkward atmosphere in the house and longed for a reconciliation with his wife. He'd been careful since that awful night. He was relieved that he'd avoided what could have been a difficult situation with regard to his client's money. He was grateful to Barbara, but it was a grudging gratefulness. It was true that he had been foolish, but he thrived on taking risks. Now he knew he must be more careful. He couldn't afford to antagonise his wife even more than he had. How was he to regain her trust? Paying back the money he owed her was a thorn in his flesh. He hated parting with his cash, but at least it was going towards a trust for his children. He stared thoughtfully into the fire as he heard footsteps coming down the stairs.

"Do you want a glass of sherry, Babs?" he called out.

The door opened and his wife entered the room looking even paler than she had earlier. There were dark shadows under her eyes and she looked drawn and haggard with tiredness. "No, thank you. I think we'd better have a talk," she said, as she stood holding on to the back of her chair.

Immediately Philip was on the defensive. "What about? I behaved myself this afternoon didn't I?"

"I'm pregnant." Barbara murmured.

"Hell. I'm sorry. I presume it's the result of that ghastly night. Oh darling, I really am so sorry." He rose from his chair and went towards Barbara, who put up her hands to ward him off.

"Please don't touch me," she said, tears streaming down her face. "I don't want it, but I suppose I'll just have to get on with it. I've felt filthy ever since that night. Why in God's name did you have to behave as you did? A part of me died that night. You killed a part of our love. I should hate you, but I still remember how much I loved you, and how happy we once were. If it wasn't for the children, I'd wish I were dead."

"Barbara, I love you. I always will and I'll be eternally sorry for what I've done to you. I've hated myself ever since. Please forgive me."

She sat down heavily in her chair. Her hand covered her face. He knelt down and put his arms round her. At first she flinched from his touch, but then relaxed as he kissed her hair.

"Please darling, for the sake of the children, and for all the happy times we've shared, can't we start again? I do so love you," he said, putting great feeling into his voice.

He stroked her hair and whispered endearments to her until she became calmer. When she had wiped her eyes and blown her nose, he got up from his kneeling position and went and poured brandy into two glasses. Handing one to her he said with a smile. "For medicinal purposes only."

"Thank you. Sorry for the outpouring. But I'm just so tired of the charade we have to play in front of everyone. I've not been sleeping well, and I've felt so depressed by all that has happened. Perhaps we can make a fresh start. But let's take things slowly please."

"Darling, I shall start courting you all over again. You are such a wonderful wife and mother. Now you just sit there and I'll go and make us an omelette for supper."

Barbara leaned back in her chair. Perhaps it would all come right.

Chapter 28

By April Barbara was six months pregnant, and for the past two months had been feeling well. Philip was very caring with her. She could not complain about his behaviour. He was very loving and she blossomed under all his attention. Things were going well in the firm too. As far as Barbara was concerned, she felt Philip had learned his lesson. But there was a lingering doubt in her mind. Ivan Jones had taken early retirement and returned to Wales. The new partner, Justin Clarke, was keen and very astute. Charming, tall, fair haired with grey-blue eyes, he was a distinct improvement on the rather dour Ivan. Justin was thirty-one, and came from a wealthy background. He was an eligible bachelor, and Helen Peterson was obviously interested in him. Barbara had her reservations about the newcomer. But she thought he would be good to have in the firm.

Michael Burgess and Jane Hart's wedding took place on the Saturday after Easter, and the reception was at the farm. Barbara had organised Mrs West to look after the children, and had bought herself a rather expensive silvery-grey dress and matching coat. She wore a fuchsia coloured hat with gloves to match.

Philip gave her a whistle of admiration when he saw her come down the stairs. "Darling, you may be six months pregnant, but you'll put Jane in the shade with that outfit. You look good enough to eat."

Barbara smiled broadly at him, and bowed her head in acknowledgement of his compliment. "Thank you, kind sir. Now we'd better get off to the church. It wouldn't do to be late."

The bride looked lovely in a white brocade dress. Instead of a veil, she wore a glorious white hat with camellias round the brim. At the reception, Barbara noticed Bill Franks on his own, looking lonely. She went across to talk to him.

"Where is Beth? I was looking forward to meeting her. How are you both?"

"Beth's in hospital, and couldn't come. We're waiting for the results of some tests. She's not been well for some time."

Placing her hand on Bill's arm, Barbara said, "Oh I am so sorry, Bill. I do hope it is nothing serious."

"I'm afraid it is. She went in to have some tests because we've been unable to have a child. They discovered she had ovarian cancer. They operated, and she's been having chemo-therapy. But she doesn't seem to be responding. I shouldn't really be here, but she insisted I come. Barbara, I'm devastated. She's so lovely. It all seems so unfair." He turned his head away and looked out onto the rolling hills beyond the farm. He laid his hand on Barbara's and squeezed it.

She bent forwards and kissed him on the cheek. "Bill, I am so very sorry. I wish there was something I could do for you both. Aunt Harriet says she is a lovely sweet person."

Across the room, Philip had watched this interplay, and was really uncomfortable. Jane had caught him on his own and had warned him not to overstep the mark again. He'd been shocked by her hostility, and it annoyed him to see Barbara talking intimately with Bill Franks. Turning aside, he grabbed another glass of champagne as a waiter passed him.

By the time the speeches were made and the cake cut, it was obvious to Barbara that Philip had had too much to drink. As soon as the married couple had left, she grabbed hold of his hand and said diplomatically. "Let's go and say our thanks and goodbyes now. My feet are killing me and I'm tired."

Once outside she insisted on driving. "Please let me drive, Philip. I've only had one glass of champagne. I'm afraid you've had more than you should to drive carefully."

"You've been counting have you?" he sneered. "I thought

you were too busy flirting with that Bill Franks you so admire, to have noticed. Your friend Jane wasn't exactly friendly towards me either. God, what a bunch of stuck-up sods they are. Here are the bloody keys. Can't have my wife and unborn child smashed up because I've had too much champagne."

"Get in Philip, and just be quiet. You've made enough of a spectacle of yourself without us having a fight in public."

She drove carefully home, and let Philip out of the car before she drove it into the garage. She hoped he might have sobered up a bit during the drive home. But she knew all the signs were that he was simmering with rage. She took time closing the garage doors, and by the time she had entered the house, he was not to be found downstairs. Mrs West met her in the hall.

"Is Mr Sharp all right?" she enquired. "He hurried up the stairs, and I heard the bedroom door slam."

Barbara smiled at her. "I think he may have had a little too much champagne, and has probably gone to sleep it off. The wedding was lovely, and we really enjoyed it. It brought back so many happy memories of almost eight years ago. It seems a lifetime."

"Wait until it's thirty years. That is a lifetime. Well, I'll be off. I'd try and rest tomorrow if I was you. You look tired now, and you looked so bonny when you left this morning. See you on Monday."

Barbara closed and locked the front door once Mrs West had gone. She walked slowly upstairs, wondering what had brought on this unnecessary verbal attack from Philip. When she opened the bedroom door, his clothes were strewn on the floor and he had collapsed naked across the bed. She covered him up with the quilt. Quietly she got her clothes for the next morning and made her way to the guest room. Little point in waking her husband up, she thought. He would be grumpy enough tomorrow. Too much champagne always gave him a monumental hangover.

Next morning, while she was giving the children their breakfast, Philip entered the kitchen with a face like thunder. It was quite plain that he was not in the best of moods.

"What would you like for breakfast this morning?" she asked.

"Black coffee and orange juice, if there is any."

"Daddy didn't say please did he? We have to," piped up Anne.

"Young madam, just be quiet," Philip snapped at his daughter. "I'm in no mood for any cheek from you."

Her lips quivered, and she looked at her mother, who shook her head at her. "If you two are finished," said Barbara, "Go and clean your teeth and play in your bedroom until I come up in a little while."

Once they had left the kitchen Barbara turned on her husband. "That was quite unnecessary. I'm trying to bring them up to be polite, and you are undermining my authority. Just because you have a hangover, do not take it out on the children. I suggest you take a couple of aspirin and stop feeling sorry for yourself."

"Oh for god's sake. I'm fed up with pussy-footing round you. I'll take my coffee through to the study and read the papers in peace. I'm going out later this morning. Don't expect me back until late tonight."

"Where are you going?" asked Barbara.

"I don't have to account to you for all my movements. I'll probably go and see my parents. I just want to get away for a few hours. Yesterday's proceedings made me realise how stultifying I find all your friends, and especially Harriet. She was nosing round me, asking questions about the firm and about us. Just because she's your relative doesn't mean she can interrogate me. She's an overpowering bitch. Not much wonder her husband left her."

Barbara's eye flashed angrily at him. "How dare you talk about Aunt Harriet like that. She's only concerned about our happiness. What's happened to make you so ill-tempered and nasty? I hate it when you're like this. I begin to wonder how we ever got into this kind of relationship. You've changed so much over the last year. I feel I no longer know you."

"I don't care what you think. I'm just fed up with you all." Gulping his coffee down quickly, he stalked out of the kitchen saying. "I'm going to Bristol now. The sooner I'm out of here, the better for us all."

Barbara felt a sense of relief when she heard the front door slam. She needed time to herself to think over what he had been saying. She'd clearly been mistaken in thinking that all was now well with their marriage. She only hoped her husband had not been guilty of fraud again. For the sake of the children, she would try and continue to cope. But what love she had felt for him had taken another knock, and she didn't think she could ever feel any affection for him again. How she would feel if he were unfaithful again, she suddenly realised that she wouldn't care. If only she weren't pregnant, she would have told him to get out. She felt hurt and abused again.

Chapter 29

There was an uneasy truce when he returned late that night. He didn't apologise, and she didn't question him about his behaviour or where he had been. Once again she told him he could sleep in the guest room, telling him she was no longer prepared to share her bed with him.

During the next few weeks, Barbara was aware that he was spending more time at the club, and was often late home. She didn't enquire as to how he occupied his time, but she had her suspicions. As long as he wasn't playing around with his client's money, she didn't really care. She was aware that her feelings for him had changed. The man she had married so many years ago was no longer visible, except when they were in the company of others.

As her pregnancy progressed, her social life decreased. She saw quite a lot of Jane, who was now working part-time in a lawyer's in Taunton. Dick Passmore was acting as chauffeur to Aunt Harriet, who came in once a week at least. Her keen eye noticed the bloom of early pregnancy had worn off her great-niece. She was now looking haggard and tired.

Harriet tried to be subtle in questioning how Barbara was feeling. "Is everything all right, my dear? You're looking so worried and unhappy. I don't like to see you looking like this. Can I do anything to help?"

Barbara was so troubled, that for once she confided to her great-aunt, "Oh, if only you could, Aunt Harriet. Philip and I seem to have drifted apart. I know I'm pregnant and look awful, but I'm just so tired of trying to make things work. Please don't say anything to Philip, but this child was not really planned or wanted. I feel I have got to tell someone. When you fell and broke your leg, we had a quarrel. He was drunk one night, and he attacked me and raped me. He needed money. He'd wrongly invested some client's money, and needed to pay it back. I refused to give it to him, and he hit me. Next day I told him I'd lend him the money but on my terms. Jane helped me draw up an agreement, and he signed it, reluctantly. When I knew I was pregnant, he apologised, and we were happy until Jane's wedding, when he got drunk again. Since then he's been so cool and distant, and takes no interest in the children. I just don't know what to do."

Harriet was furious, but she promised that she wouldn't do anything to jeopardise the marriage further. When next she saw Jane Burgess, she let her know that Barbara had informed her about the situation. They decided between them that they would do all they could to alleviate the state of affairs.

Early in June, Philip announced that he was going up to London for a conference. He would be gone three days, and would telephone in the evenings. He left early on the Wednesday morning.

On the Thursday afternoon Jane called round on her way home, and found Barbara white-faced and in pain. The baby wasn't due for another four weeks, but it was clear that her friend was in labour. Jane phoned Mrs West, and arranged for her to pick up the children from school, while she took Barbara to the hospital. Having seen Barbara safely into the hospital, she waited until the doctor had examined her friend.

"I am afraid that it's a breech presentation, and we'll have to try and turn the baby. Mrs Sharp is in a great deal of pain at present, and is becoming distressed. Can you get in touch with her husband? He should be here for her."

"I'm sorry," said Jane, "But he's in London at present attending a conference. I'll see if I can get some information from his colleagues. They may know where he's staying and could get in touch with him. Tell Mrs Sharp I'll look after her children. I'll also phone her great-aunt who lives at

Stickleburn, and let her know what's happened."

The doctor was obviously worried. "If we can't turn the baby, we may have to do a Caesarean operation. Mrs Sharp's blood pressure is very high at present, and I'm not happy about her condition."

Jane left the hospital feeling very apprehensive. When she returned to the Sharps' house, she found Mrs West coping with the children. Both women decided that it would be a good idea for Jane to take the children home with her for a few days. Jane got in touch with Philip's partner Samuel Peterson, who had no idea that Philip was in London. He knew nothing about a conference, and neither did Justin Clarke. All they knew was that Philip had taken three days off. They promised to try to find out where he'd gone. Jane was very angry, but didn't dare show her anger in front of Mrs West and the children. She asked Mrs West to pack some clothes for the children, while she phoned Mrs Tremayne.

Harriet was furious when she knew that Philip was out of contact. She told Jane that she would get Dick Passmore to bring her into Taunton immediately. "Please leave the key where I can get at it. I can't have Barbara facing this on her own. Thanks, Jane, for taking the children. I could cheerfully kill that rotten husband of hers. I'll keep in touch with you."

Jane drove home to the farm with the children, and Michael welcomed them gladly. He suggested they might help him feed the hens.

Harriet meanwhile was driven into the hospital, where she managed to get the registrar to give her the latest new of her great-niece's condition. They had been unsuccessful in trying to turn the baby, and Barbara had just been given a sedative, prior to being taken into theatre. Harriet was taken in to see Barbara, and was able to tell her that the children were being cared for by Jane, and that they were trying to get in touch with Philip. Barbara slowly moved her head and in a low whisper said that she couldn't care less where he was.

The registrar suggested to Harriet that she get some rest. She decided to go to Barbara's home. Dick would stay with her. They entered the house, and were sitting having a cup of tea in the kitchen when the phone rang.

"Hello Barbara," said Philip.

"Where the hell are you?" an angry Harriet demanded. "We've been trying to get in touch with you. No-one knew where you were, and don't tell me it was a conference. Your partners said you'd taken some time off. I suggest you get back here as soon as you can. Barbara's in hospital and due to have a Caesarean. The baby is in the breech position, and they can't turn it. She's very sick, and you are not here to give her your support. Actually, she said she couldn't care less about you when I saw her about half an hour ago."

"Oh dear Lord. I didn't think anything like this would occur. I'll see if I can get a train tonight. Give her my love if you are going in. I'm really sorry."

"So you should be. You've played around once too often for my liking. Barbara doesn't deserve to be treated to your rotten behaviour. Get back here as quickly as you can." Harriet put the phone down, and went back to the kitchen where Dick was sitting waiting for her. He took one look at her face and suggested she could do with something a bit stronger than tea. She told him where the brandy was kept, and he poured her a small glass which she drank while he finished his tea.

About eleven o'clock the phone rang. It was the registrar, and he sounded anxious. "Mrs Sharp is all right, but I am afraid there is something wrong with the baby. I think you should get over here as soon as you can, please. Any sign of her husband yet?"

"I've managed to contact him, and he's coming back as soon as he can."

The clinical antiseptic smell assailed Harriet's nostrils as she opened the door to the ward. How she hated hospitals. They reminded her of the time Barbara's parents had been killed. She made her way wearily to the cubicle at the end. She was aware of the wailing of babies in cots beside their mothers. She vaguely noticed the décor of the ward – pale green with faded flowered curtains, which had shrunk in the cleaning, as the hems had been let down but not sewn.

On reaching the cubicle, she saw that a white-faced Barbara was lying in the bed with a saline drip attached to a cannula on her left hand. A nurse was standing by the bed as Harriet went towards her great niece.

"Oh Mrs Tremayne," she said, "I'm glad that you're here. We've been so anxious about Mrs Sharp. She's taken the news of the baby's condition badly. She has really had a bad confinement and is very weak. Any news of her husband coming? He should be here for her."

"I've been in touch with him. I believe he was up in London. He phoned about an hour ago and said he'd catch the first train back. Where is the baby?"

"The baby is in an incubator at present. She was over five pounds in weight, but she had difficulty breathing. She is definitely suffering from Down's syndrome, and the doctor decided it would be safer to place the child in the incubator. He also felt it would be best to let Mrs Sharp get over the shock before letting her see the child. Although she has recovered from the anaesthetic, she's gone to sleep again."

The nurse checked the drip, before placing a chair near the bed for Harriet. "Would you like a cup of tea? You may have a while to wait until your great-niece wakes up."

Harriet smiled at the girl as she said. "I'd rather have a stiff brandy, but a cup of tea will do for the present. Thank you my dear."

Chapter 30

Harriet sank gratefully into the chair. Her emotions were confused. Pity for Barbara and the child, and anger and fury at Philip, who she suspected had gone to London to amuse himself. From the beginning, she had never really trusted him, and she was quite sure that he'd married Barbara for her money. But she'd known that if she had objected to him, Barbara would still have gone her own way and married him. She had been besotted with him. Harriet had for some time had a suspicion that all was not well with the marriage, and Barbara had confirmed it only the other week. Philip had been extremely evasive and distant on the few occasions she had seen him. She wondered what she could do to help. She loved Barbara dearly and was extremely fond of young David and Anne, who she felt were being used as pawns in the marriage. She had to be strong for Barbara, but she was unsure of how she could resolve the problem of Philip.

The nurse handing her a cup of tea roused her from her thoughts. "As Mr Sharp is not available, Dr Robbins would like to explain the situation to you, Mrs Tremayne. Perhaps once you've had your tea, you could come to Sister's office."

"Yes, certainly, my dear. Thank you for the tea. I won't be long."

Harriet took a few sips of the tea, and then got up slowly from the chair, and made her way to the Sister's station. At seventy-three, she was beginning to realise that she was no longer as fit as she would like to be. She hated the aches and creaks that her body gave her, and she hated the thought that one day she would probably have to give up her independence. It was a grim thought, and it was with a sinking feeling that she knocked on the door.

Doctor Robbins rose from behind the desk and held out his

hand to Harriet. "I am so sorry. This will be a terrible blow to your great-niece and her husband."

"Never mind her husband," said Harriet crossly, "It's Barbara I am worried about, and how she's going to cope."

Doctor Robbins gently explained that the baby was definitely a Down's syndrome child, with a heart defect. He felt there was a chance that the child might not survive, as she was having breathing difficulties. Certainly, she would need a lot of care and nursing. At present he felt that Barbara was so exhausted she couldn't cope. He suggested that once Barbara had recovered from the birth, the child should be left in the hospital until they had a better idea whether her condition would improve or not.

Harriet agreed with the doctor. There was no way of knowing how Barbara would cope with a sickly and handicapped baby. "Thank you, Doctor Robbins. I'll go and sit with my great-niece until she wakes. She needs someone to care for her."

"You look as if you could do with some rest yourself. I'll get the nurse to bring a pillow and blanket for you, so that you can perhaps sleep beside Mrs Sharp."

Harriet returned to the cubicle, and as she sat down Barbara gave a deep sigh. It was almost a moan. Her eyelids fluttered and opened. There was a blank look in the eyes for a few seconds. Then a look of horror appeared on her face as she became conscious of where she was. Her head turned on the pillow and she caught sight of her great-aunt. Immediately tears trickled down her cheeks as Harriet leant over to kiss her and take her hand.

"Aunt Harriet," she said softly, "What am I going to do? How will Philip take this awful news? Everything has got to be perfect for him. He'll leave us. I know he will. Where is he? Why isn't he here?" She was becoming hysterical.

Luckily, the nurse heard and came into the cubicle. She

tried to calm her patient. "You're very tired, Mrs Sharp, and no doubt in pain after the operation. I'll go and ask if you can have some medication for the pain."

As she turned to go there was a commotion at the entrance to the ward. Harriet recognised Philip's angry voice saying, "Where is she? I want to see her immediately!"

Doctor Robbins had his hand on Philip's arm as if restraining him from making too much noise. "Mr Sharp. It is four o'clock in the morning. Please have some consideration for the patients who are in this ward. Please be calm. Come into the office. Your wife is recovering from a rather traumatic confinement. We had to do a Caesar and I'm afraid the baby is handicapped. You are not going to help matters by being so aggressive. Mrs Tremayne is with your wife at present, as we couldn't contact you."

Philip quickly decided he'd better not make a scene. His guilt at having been absent and unattainable made him realise it would put him at a disadvantage. He'd not wanted this child, and knew it was the result of his appalling behaviour that night he had raped his wife. He had felt ashamed of himself afterwards, and it had put a strain on his marriage. He'd had to grovel to Barbara. But he'd been desperate to clear his debts before they were exposed. Something had definitely gone out of the marriage, and he knew he was to blame. Taking a deep breath, he turned to Doctor Robbins and apologised. "I'm sorry. It is just that I should have been here for her. I had to go to this meeting and ..."

Doctor Robbins interrupted him saying, "Now that you are here, I'd better explain the situation. Then you can see your wife. But I warn you, she is in a state of shock and very exhausted, so you mustn't stay long."

Philip's shoulders straightened as he followed the doctor into the small office. On being informed of what had happened, he was shattered. The thought of having to cope with a handicapped child horrified him. Better, he thought if the child had died. But he couldn't say this to anyone.

"Please may I see Barbara now? I promise I'll not stay too long."

"Do you wish to see the baby?"

"Not at present. I don't think I could bear to yet. Has Barbara seen it?"

"No. We thought it better if she didn't. When she's stronger, perhaps she'll ask to see her daughter."

Doctor Robbins accompanied him along to his wife's cubicle. Harriet looked up as he entered. She stared icily at him.

Philip leaned over Barbara and kissed her forehead. Her eyes fluttered open and she turned her face from him.

"Darling I'm sorry I wasn't here for you," he whispered.

"Just leave me alone please," she said, in a weak voice.

Doctor Robbins put his hand on Philip's shoulder saying, "I think we should leave her at present. She's just had some further sedation. If there's any change, we'll phone you. I suggest you take Mrs Tremayne home. She's been here most of the time, and she must be tired."

Harriet rose from her chair and, ignoring Philip, she made her way out of the cubicle and out of the ward. Philip was frightened by her demeanour and felt he had to hurry after her. He caught up with her in the entrance hall. "What are we going to do, Harriet? I should have been here."

"Yes. You bloody well should have been. I will do what I can to help Barbara and the little one. As for you, you'd better try and salvage your marriage, before it's too late. I know Barbara has helped you out of debt at least once. Do not let it happen again. I blame you for this disaster, and it will be a long time before I forget – if ever. Your children are being looked after by Jane Burgess at present, and you'd better leave them there for the time being. At least they are not in the line of fire."

She turned from him and made her way to where Dick Passmore had parked her car. Dick had been waiting in the entrance hall all the time, and was worried about the old lady. He and his wife were devoted to her, and as he followed Harriet to the car, he glared at Philip, who was stunned by all that had happened to him in the last two days. He watched as Harriet slammed her car door and was driven out of his sight.

Chapter 31

Within a few days Barbara was beginning to recover from the operation and the distress caused by the baby's difficult birth. She had asked to see the baby on the second day. As she held the child in her arms and gazed at the fuzz of golden hair and the small face with slanting eyes, she felt a rush of tenderness towards the babe. Her feelings at first being told that the child suffered from Down's syndrome had been of horror and revulsion. Now she only felt love and pity.

Without discussion with Philip, she arranged for the baby to be christened Megan. The hospital padre carried out the ceremony, when Harriet was visiting one afternoon. The paediatrician had informed Barbara that the baby was still in a critical condition and would require to be monitored for some time. That was the reason Barbara decided on the baptism taking place.

Since his hasty return from London, Philip had tried desperately hard to ingratiate himself with his wife. But she had enough to cope with without her husband attempting to show everyone how attentive he was towards her. She knew by now that he'd been in London for his own amusement, and not, as he had told her, to attend a conference. That knowledge made her all the more determined that his present attitude and consideration was not going to hold any sway over her.

Little Megan's condition improved once she had bonded with her mother, but there was still the worry about her heart condition. It was decided to leave her in the hospital until she was stronger. Eventually they hoped to operate on her, but for now it would be best if the child was left in professional hands.

Barbara returned home two weeks after Megan's birth.

Philip took it for granted that he would sleep in the marital bed, and was most upset when Barbara told him that he was not welcome.

"But darling, we really need to be together. I do love you."

"So you've often told me. But I am afraid that I no longer believe you. I'm fed up with all your playing around, and at present I'm too tired and depressed by all that's happened over the past year. By the way, I will require more help when Megan comes home. Have you any suggestions? Your parents, bless them, have been very supportive and sympathetic, and they have offered to help. Your father even suggested that they'd like to move nearer to us, now that he'as retired."

"That would be good for us all," answered Philip, "But I doubt they could afford to buy a house near us."

"I'm not suggesting they do. I thought we could turn the basement into a flat for them. In fact, I've drawn a plan that I think could be feasible. There's enough space for three rooms, plus a kitchen and bathroom, and they could have their own front door at the back of the house."

A look of amazement came over Philip's face. She had obviously planned it all out already. "But it'll cost rather a lot to have all the work carried out won't it? And where am I going to find that sort of money?"

"I'm not suggesting you should spend anything. I doubt if you've got much in the way of savings anyway. God knows how much you have these days. I'll get Mr McGrath to arrange for the architect and builder to come and give us an estimate. I feel sure he'll approve. Aunt Harriet is agreeable."

"You've discussed it with her before sounding me out. She always come before me, blast her."

"That's because she always has my interests at heart. Something you don't seem to bother about lately. Please do not let us argue. I'm tired and going to bed. We'll discuss it later when I've seen Mr McGrath."

Philip's face was flushed with anger. He was beginning to see that instead of the weak and malleable innocent young girl he thought he'd married, his wife had discovered great strength of character, and the ability to cope when hit by adversity. All right, she was wealthy and didn't have to worry about money. But for all her wealth, she was unspoiled. If his parents did come to live in the basement, it would certainly be a help as far as Megan was concerned. His mother was a sensible woman, who'd been a nurse before she married, and his father liked gardening. He decided that it was an excellent idea. But he would have to be discreet about his extra marital affairs. He knew neither of his parents would approve. He smiled wryly to himself.

As soon as Barbara had talked to Jack and Meg Sharp about the plans, they had agreed to sell up and move down as soon as possible. An architect looked at Barbara's rough drawings. Then he set to work to plan the transformation of the basement into a three-roomed flat. He had quite a number of suggestions to make, and costed it all out. Planning permission was granted. With the agreement of Harriet and Mr McGrath, it was decided work should start immediately.

The Sharps' house in Bristol was quickly sold. Barbara then realised that Jack and Meg would have to move down before the flat was ready for occupation. That meant she and Philip would have to share a room again. She was quite adamant that she could not share a bed with him, and ordered two single beds to be delivered. Without discussion, she decided that one of the attic rooms would be turned into another bedroom where the double bed could go. After all, the children were growing, and would soon require separate rooms.

When Philip learned what she was proposing, he was annoyed that he'd not been consulted. "This is my home too, you know," he said to her one evening.

"I don't deny that it is your home, but you don't own it. I'd remind you that it is in trust for the children, and that any money I decide to spend on it will add to the value for them."

"You never let me forget that do you? We are husband and wife. Twin beds in our room? What will my parents think?"

"You can tell them I'm a restless sleeper, and that I thought twin beds would mean you wouldn't be disturbed. After all, dear, you do need your sleep don't you?" Barbara said ironically. "You have to work so late at night."

"Please can't we call a truce? I know I've been no angel. But I am trying to care for you now."

"We can be civilised about it all," she replied, "But I'm afraid my love for you has diminished over the years. I no longer feel that I want you to make love to me. As long as you are discreet, you can have your affairs. But I don't want your parents or the children to suspect anything. We'll continue as we are until the children are older. I do not want them hurt. Megan will be home in two weeks, and I'll be kept busy looking after her. You don't seem to show any interest in her at all."

"How can I? She's severely handicapped, and I've always avoided contact with handicapped people. It would have been better if she'd been stillborn."

"You mean better for you. Then you wouldn't have had to live with the guilt. Is that it? Does it make you feel that God is punishing you for raping your wife? But I doubt if you believe in God."

"You really are becoming hard and cynical Barbara. I thought I knew you very well. But I don't now. I'm confused by your bitterness."

"I'm just as confused by the fact that you've been unfaithful, and by your conduct over the past year or so. I was very much in love with you when we were first married. You changed just before Anne was born, and since then things have steadily deteriorated. When you hit me last November, something died inside me. Now that I know you've had numerous affairs, I'm afraid that love has sometimes been replaced by hatred. Perhaps one day I may be able to forgive you. But not at present."

She turned from him to continue hanging curtains in the attic bedroom.

The baby was almost four months old when she was finally brought home. The paediatrician had decided to wait until she was older before operating on her heart. Barbara had visited her in hospital every day and watched as the nurses dealt with her. She was a placid baby who only cried when she was hungry. Then she would go red in the face and start to turn blue. Barbara had taken notice of how the nurses coped. At times she was very afraid and depressed, but the sight of her handicapped child gave her the strength and determination required.

Jack and Meg Sharp had arrived two days previously, and had settled into the spare room until the basement flat was ready. They had stored their furniture, and they were both delighted with the progress that had been made. Their living room and one bedroom looked out to the back garden, with views over the lawn and rose garden to the green hills beyond. The other bedroom, bathroom and kitchen were actually at the front of the house, with a small path running under the steps to the main front door. Their own front door was at the back.

The builders reckoned on completing all the work and decoration by the end of November. Meg was pleased at the thought that they would be settled in by Christmas, and so give Philip and Barbara privacy. She was amazed at how well Barbara was dealing with Megan. She also noticed that Philip ignored the tiny mite. It was as if the child didn't exist as far as he was concerned. She was extremely upset by his attitude, but apart from mentioning it to her husband, she kept her mouth shut.

By Christmas, they'd all settled into a routine. During the day Meg was there to look after Megan when Barbara had to take David and Anne to school and when she went shopping or to visit her great-aunt. But Barbara did not seem to want to go out to visit friends. Jane would call and see how everybody was, but Barbara wasn't interested in anyone else.

Jack kept himself busy in the garden, and spent hours in the greenhouse. It was a novelty to him to have so much space to himself. In Bristol they'd had such a small garden, and it had always been his ambition to have a bigger one. He was in his element. He loved having the grandchildren about him, and would spend time with Megan, singing to her in his baritone voice. She would smile up at him and wiggle her little feet in pleasure.

Christmas seemed to be a very happy time for them all. Even Barbara enjoyed watching the progress Megan had made, and was very grateful to her parents-in-law for being so helpful. From being afraid of Meg when she was first married, she had developed a love for her, and great respect for the way she coped with Megan. David and Anne thrived on all the attention they got from their grandparents.

In the New Year, the firm of Mead, Jones and Peterson decided that they would have to expand their offices. The practice had grown so much as the town grew in size. There was talk of taking on another partner as well. Philip was working hard, and making sure that he did not gamble with his client's money these days. He was playing it safe. Also, with his parents living in the flat, he had told Helen Peterson that they could not continue their affair, which had been going on for some considerable time. She had been the reason he'd gone to London, and he felt very guilty whenever he saw her.

She'd been furious when he told her it all had to stop. But she'd turned her attention to Justin Clarke, and for a while all had been well. Now Justin had just announced his engagement to a vivacious redhead whose parents owned a large manor house north of Taunton. Philip was afraid that Helen might make trouble. How she managed to conceal all her affairs from her husband was a mystery. But as long as she left him alone he was happy.

Chapter 32

Megan grew into a happy loving child. She could, on occasion, throw tantrums that disrupted the household. Her little face would grow puce with rage and frustration, and Barbara would be quite exhausted by the time the tantrum had run its course. Meg was wonderful with her little grandchild. She could calm the child with remarkable ease. Anne, by now a child of eight, had infinite patience with her handicapped sister, who eagerly awaited her return from school.

David loved Megan too, but at ten he was more interested in sports. He was tall for his age and very perceptive to all the various moods that prevailed in the house. He was close to his grandfather, who went to watch him play cricket or football for his school. Philip rarely took any interest in the children, except when the end of term reports arrived. Then he would berate his son if his work were below standard.

The young boy sensed that all was not well between his parents. He had overheard arguments at times, and intuitively knew when it was best to keep a low profile. He was popular at school and had lots of friends. He also loved Aunt Harriet, and was always keen to visit her. On one occasion when the atmosphere at home had been really fraught, he had caught a bus to Minehead and then to Stickleburn. He told Harriet, "Mum and Dad have had a right old set-to, and I just felt I wanted to come to you. You always make me feel safe. I just wish Dad didn't pick on Mum so much. Sometimes it's as if she can't do anything right, and ends up crying in her room. I just seem to make things worse if Dad catches sight of me."

This troubled Harriet and when she phoned Barbara she told her what he had said. "Both of you will have to be more careful in future," she added, "I'll keep him here until Sunday. But I think you would be wise to send him away to a boarding school in a year or two. It's not good for him to be caught in the crossfire."

"I agree Aunt Harriet," replied Barbara. "I'll try and have a serious talk with Philip about it. It isn't fair that David should be so upset. But my dear husband is enough to make a saint swear at times. I've a feeling he's playing away again. Trips to Bristol and late nights. I don't want his parents hurt by his behaviour, but Meg is beginning to suspect. She asked me the other day why Philip is away so much. I had to make the excuse that it was all to do with the business. I'm so tired of the charade that we put on for everyone. But what can I do?"

"Not much at present, my dear. You'll have to have proof. It may come sooner than you think."

"Why do you say that?" asked Barbara.

"I was talking to Jane the other day, and she said that Michael had told her there was some gossip that Philip was seen with some local woman in Bristol about a month ago. But Michael didn't say who the woman was, or if he did know, he didn't tell Jane. Bill Franks was here this last weekend and was asking about you. He is kept busy at the hospital, which is just as well. He took Beth's death very badly. She had suffered so much."

"I'd like to see Bill again. He looked so tired and lost the last time I saw him. I'll have to speak to Jane, and see if we can get together sometime. I gather Jane's twins are creating havoc at times. She said she'll be glad when they go to school. Thanks for phoning and letting me know that David's with you. I was very worried. I'll come and fetch him on Sunday afternoon. Give him my love and say that things will be calmer at home."

Barbara replaced the receiver and stood in contemplation in the hall for a few moments. She was thinking about Bill and how tired he had looked when she last saw him. After

Beth's death he had sold the house in Norton Fitzwarren and moved into a flat in Taunton near the hospital. He and his cousin Michael Burgess had always been close, and Barbara knew that Jane and Michael kept a careful eye on him. It was now two years since Beth had died, and Bill just seemed to live for his work. She remembered that although he had looked tired, he had been obviously pleased to see her. They had always been very easy together.

Philip came out of the study and looked at her warily. He had been extremely annoyed with David for running away. Angry and anxious and also guilty, because he knew that the boy had overheard the quarrel he'd had with his wife.

"Well, what was all that about?" he queried.

Barbara told him that David was with Harriet.

"Another member of the family who prefers her to me," he snapped.

"Is it any wonder? He heard us this morning and was upset. Look, Philip, let's go and talk this over in comfort. It's about time we tried to stop all the angst. It's affecting the children, and your mother has noticed we're not really happy in each other's company."

Following Barbara into the study, Philip thought that she was right. He had been bitter and resentful ever since Barbara had bailed him out of trouble almost six years ago. He hated the fact that he was beholden to her for so much. The house, her money, and all she had done for his parents. David running away had shaken him more than he cared for. His own son pushed too far by the behaviour of his father. Because he knew that it was his bitterness that caused him to act as he did.

"Well, what do you suggest we do?" he asked, as he closed the study door.

"Can we try harder to be civil to each other? It's as if a word or a gesture is enough to spark a row, and next minute we're at each other's throats. I know it hasn't been easy since Megan was born, but she is such a happy child. She does demand a lot of attention from us all. Perhaps once the holidays are over and she starts at the play group this next term, I won't be so tied down during the day. Then we may have more time to spend together. We must try for the sake of the children and also for ourselves. It's wrecking any chance for our marriage. I know I've not been easy to live with since Megan arrived. But then neither have you. But I will try harder in future if you will."

"Barbara, I'll try too. If only we can forget the past. I know I've been mainly to blame. I've been so bitter since that awful night. Could you really try and forgive me please?" he begged.

"I think I've forgiven you, but I doubt if I'll ever forget. Probably just as well. I'm wary of you Philip, but I'm still fond of you in a way, and you are the father of my children."

She went towards him and for the first time in years she intuitively put her arms round him and reached up to kiss him on the cheek. He was startled by her action, but he bent his head and their lips met. Barbara was aware that her feelings for her husband had never really disappeared, and she returned his kiss eagerly.

"Darling, I suppose I've never stopped loving you," she said breathlessly.

"Thank God for that, my love." His hands roved over her body and he felt his passion aroused. "This needs celebrating. Why don't you go upstairs and I'll get a bottle of wine and some glasses?"

Barbara went upstairs, and looked in on Anne and Megan, who were sleeping peacefully. She gently stroked Megan's fair hair. Love for the little girl welled up inside her. She may have been unwanted before she was born, but now she was so much a part of Barbara's life, that every day she was alive seemed like a bonus. She knew that one day soon they would have to face up to the fact that she had to have the operation on her heart. She feared for what lay ahead for the little one.

As she turned to go to her own room, she saw her husband hovering in the door watching her.

"You really do love that little scrap don't you?" he remarked.

"Yes Philip, I do. It's quite different from the love I feel for David and Anne. I feel protective love towards her, and she repays me in so many ways. Bless her."

"You are a good mother. I only wish I could have been as good a father to them all. But I'm afraid I'm flawed in some way."

They moved towards their own room and Philip put the tray containing the wine and glasses on to the bedside table. He watched Barbara as she undressed in front of the dressing table. He put his arms round her and whispered gently in her ears. "Your bed or mine?"

Barbara smiled and turned round to face him, starting to undo the buttons of his shirt. "Does it really matter?" she said.

Chapter 33

Barbara drove to Stickleburn on the Sunday afternoon to pick up David. Megan, who was strapped into a seat in the back, accompanied her. She loved being in the car, and was happily chatting away to herself as she looked out at the animals in the fields. On arrival, she tottered into the house to be swept up into David's arms, chuckling gaily at being united with her brother. She then hobbled to see Harriet who always made a fuss of her. The child thrived on love and attention.

David looked apprehensively at his mother. She smiled reassuringly at him. "It's all right David. Daddy and I have settled our differences, and have agreed we've been naughty to shout at each other so much. We are much happier now'.

His face cleared as he asked, "Why were you quarrelling so much? I hate it when you do, and it upsets Anne and Megan. Please be nice to each other."

Barbara put her arms round him and kissed him. She felt her heart would break at the unhappiness she and Philip had caused their children to suffer. "David, son. We love you all very much, but we don't always agree with each other. You quarrel with Anne at times don't you? So you must try and understand that when either Daddy or I are tired or worried we become angry at each other. We are going to try and be more caring in the future. Come on darling, let's have some tea with Aunt Harriet and then we'll go home."

"Where's Anne? I thought she might have come with you."

"She is spending the day with Peggy Bertram. We'll pick her up on the way back."

They went into the kitchen, where Harriet was making a pot of tea.

"Carry the tray in for me will you please Barbara? David,

will you pour some milk for Megan and yourself? There is a plate of biscuits on the table here. I'd like a few minutes with Mummy while we have our tea. Can you look after Megan?'

"All right Aunt Harriet. I'll take her to see the kittens in the barn after if that's all right with you?"

"Thank you, David, you are a dear boy."

Barbara carried the tray into the sitting-room and Harriet sat down in her comfortable old chair with a sigh of relief.

"I'm sorry, Aunt Harriet, for all the worry we've caused you. David running away has made us realise how childish we were. We were thinking only of ourselves, not of the effect our rows were having on the children. We've talked it out, and there has been reconciliation. I'm sure we'll be more careful in future. We mustn't upset the children again"

"I sincerely hope not," said Harriet coolly. "Philip has caused enough trouble already. But I doubt if he'll change much. A leopard doesn't change his spots overnight – if ever. He has caused you a lot of heartache over the years"

"I know and I've made him pay for it. It shook him when I went to Jane that time, and he knows that I'm not a soft touch any more."

"Well Barbara I would still be wary of him. You've only another year or so before you inherit the rest of your parents' money. Please be careful. David knows how bad-tempered his father can be, and has told me he is very frightened of him at times. I have a feeling he knows a lot more than he's letting on."

Barbara's eyes were filling up with unshed tears. She sniffed before answering, "Yes, I think he does. I wonder if he's heard something at school about Philip's affairs. I forget how grown up he seems to have become in this last year. He's very protective towards Anne and Megan. I've noticed he seems to sense when there's a row brewing, and takes them out of our way. We'll have to try harder at making our marriage work."

They talked until David returned with Megan, whose little eyes beamed at them. "Puddy tat pretty. Me like one," said the little girl.

"Well sweetheart. Perhaps later on. They are too young yet to leave their mummy. Come and kiss me before you go," said Harriet.

They said their farewells to Harriet. Barbara noticed how frail and old her great-aunt had become, and she felt guilty at causing her so much grief. "Thank you for being such a wonderful caring auntie to me. What would I do without you? Bless you, do take care of yourself. We'll come over during the holidays to see you. Aren't the Passmores going up to see their daughter sometime?"

"Yes, but not until the New Year," said Harriet.

"Come and stay with us while they are away. I don't like the idea of you being left on your own."

"We'll see."

Harriet waved her hand at the car as Barbara drove off. She shook her head as she closed the front door. She didn't believe Philip would behave himself. She had no intention of going to stay with Barbara for the New Year celebrations. The less she saw of her great-niece's husband the better. She'd always been suspicious of him, and wouldn't trust him at all. She knew Barbara would endeavour to keep the peace, but she also knew that the rumours she'd heard about Philip and his affairs were true, and she was certain he would continue to misbehave.

As she sat down in her chair she sighed. She suddenly felt very old, and she was worried about the future for Barbara and the children. When Barbara inherited her parents' money, she would be a very rich woman, and when Harriet herself died she would be even richer. Philip was greedy for money, and Harriet knew he would do anything to acquire money for himself. She just didn't trust him at all. But there was nothing more she could do about it at present. She knew that her will was in safe hands and that there was no way he could get his greedy hands on what she left. She had tied it all up securely.

"I feel I could do with a good strong brandy," she said aloud, and went to pour herself one.

Chapter 34

Christmas that year was a happy one for the family. The atmosphere in the house had been calm and peaceful for the last few months. Barbara felt her marriage was stronger and Philip certainly did his best to make sure that he spent quality time with David and Anne. He still couldn't show much love or affection for Megan. The grandparents were a tower of strength to Barbara. Meg adored caring for her little handicapped granddaughter. There was a special bond between them.

The only blot on the horizon was Aunt Harriet's health. She had caught a cold before Christmas which had developed into bronchitis. As a result she had been unable to attend the Christmas festivities with the family.

Jane and Michael Burgess had kept an eye on her, and of course she had the Passmores to help in the house and garden. They had made plans to visit their daughter in Gloucester for the New Year. When Barbara learned that they intended to cancel their plans, she suggested that she would come over to Stickleburn to look after her great-aunt. Jane phoned to say that she would have David and Anne to stay with her. They would happily play with their twin boys, and Barbara was grateful for the offer.

"With only Megan to cope with, it will be much easier," she confided. "Philip's parents are going up to Yorkshire to their daughter for New Year. He can cope on his own for a few days. There's plenty for him to do here, and he'll have peace and quiet. Jane, you are a godsend. See you in a couple of days."

She quickly phoned her great-aunt and spoke to Mrs Passmore who was delighted. She would prepare the rooms for Megan and Barbara, and would make sure the freezer was full of food already prepared, so that Barbara didn't have to do much in the way of cooking. "Mrs Tremayne is much better and is looking forward to seeing you. She's able to come downstairs now, and is beginning to get her appetite back. She's been eating like a sparrow until yesterday. Your visit will be a real tonic for her."

Philip was taken aback by all the plans, but was quite amenable about it. "I had hoped we could have had a party here on New Year's Eve. But it doesn't matter. I have enough to keep me busy anyway. There is a stack of work in the office I can bring home and attend to. I'll probably play some golf too, if the weather's reasonable."

On the morning of the thirtieth of December, Barbara drove across to her great-aunt's house. She deposited David and Anne at the farm. The Passmores were ready to depart. Harriet had loaned them her car so they didn't have to worry about transport to Gloucester. She wasn't going to need the car while Barbara and Megan were staying with her. Looking pale and thin, her face was smiling as her great-great-niece embraced her.

"Where's puddy tat aunty?" the little girl asked.

"Well the mummy one is in the kitchen along with one of her kittens. We've managed to find homes for the other two"

"Go see them please?"

"Mummy will take you through in a little while. Just let us get our breath back please."

Barbara smiled at the sight of her daughter and her great-aunt together. Megan seemed to have the knack of being in tune with elderly people, and they all reciprocated the feeling. "I'll just take our cases upstairs, Megan, and then I'll take you through to the kitchen and we'll all have a drink. I'll only be a minute or two. Oh, it is lovely to be here with you, Aunt Harriet."

Giving her great-aunt a hug and a kiss, she then went to

carry the cases and her handbag to her old room. Quickly she put them on the bed and made her way downstairs again.

"Sherry?" she asked her great-aunt.

"Need you ask?" came the reply.

"Come on Megan. Let's go and see the kitten and get Aunt Harriet and mummy a drink shall we? Then we can have lunch in a little while, and you can have a rest afterwards."

"Awight. Play with puddy tat in here?"

"No, I don't think so sweetie. He's only little, and we don't want puddles on the carpet do we? Once he's housetrained, perhaps he'ill be allowed in the sitting room."

She took her daughter's hand, and slowly they made their way to the kitchen. Megan was still not strong enough to undergo the operation for the hole in her heart. So the little child could not run about and be too boisterous. Her little face lit up in delight at seeing the small ginger striped kitten snuggled up in his mother's basket. Gently she stroked him and was rewarded with a lick and a purring sound.

Barbara poured two glasses of sherry and put them on a silver tray to carry through to the sitting room. "Do you want a drink, darling?" she asked Megan.

"No tank you. Me play wit puddy tat please?"

"I'll just prop the kitchen door open, so you can come through if you want to. Promise me you won't touch anything but the kitten and Poppy."

"Yes pwomise. Me be happy."

Returning to the sitting-room, she handed her great-aunt the glass of sherry, and sat down on the floor beside the fire where she could watch the old lady as they spoke. She noticed that her great-aunt's face looked lined and grey. She was frightened by what she saw. It was as if the woman had aged ten years since she last saw her. Please God, let her recover. What on earth would I do without her, she thought. The two women sipped their sherry and talked of old friends.

"I hear that Bill Franks is coming down for New Year with Jane and Michael," said Harriet. "He's promised to look in and see me. In fact Jane would like us to go over on New Year's Day for lunch. I said I didn't think that I could manage it, but that you and Megan would certainly go."

"We'll see how things go. I don't like leaving you on your own."

"I'll be all right. If you give me my lunch on a tray before you go, I'll rest in the afternoon. It would do you good to have some young company. I promise I'll behave. I'm feeling much better, darling. Let's have some lunch, and then Megan can have a rest and so can I."

Next day, while Barbara was getting lunch ready, the front doorbell rang. Standing on the step with David and Anne was Bill Franks.

"Come in Bill. How nice to see you. Harriet is in the sitting-room."

Bill put his hands on Barbara's shoulders and kissed her cheek. A warm glow ran through her and she felt her face flush as she smiled at him.

"I gather she's almost over the bronchitis," he said. "David and Anne expressed a wish to come and see her, and I offered to drive them over. Not that I need an excuse. I usually call in and see her when I'm here. I haven't seen you for quite a time. Are you happy?"

"Yes Bill. I rather think that Jane will have told you of my problems. But we seem to have resolved them for now. We had a most enjoyable Christmas."

David and Anne had already kissed Aunt Harriet and were now running through to the kitchen to see Megan and the kitten.

"Keep an eye on her will you please while Uncle Bill and I have a chat with Aunt Harriet?" said Barbara to them, "I'll be through in a minute to give you all a drink."

"Bill, how nice of you to come and visit an old lady. Give me a kiss," said Harriet, when he entered the room.

"Gladly. You may be an old lady, but you are a charming old lady."

"I bet you say that to all your elderly patients."

"No. Only to my favourite one."

Barbara noticed how easy they were in each other's company, and felt a pang of jealousy. Why couldn't Philip have that rapport with her great-aunt? She also wished that she and Bill had that same rapport. He really was so nice, and she knew she'd always been extremely fond of him. In fact she remembered that at eighteen she had loved him. Mentally she shrugged the thought away. Then she heard him enter the kitchen, and she felt that glow again. How silly was she getting? Just because she'd had a crush on him years ago shouldn't make her feel this way.

"How about a glass of sherry?" she asked, as brightly as she could. "Or would you prefer some whisky, Bill?"

"Dry sherry would be lovely, thank you, Barbara." He gave her a big smile that told her he was happy to see her. "Can I help in any way?" he added.

"No thanks Bill. I'll attend to the children, and be with you in just a minute."

She closed the door behind her, and with mixed emotions, made her way to the cupboard to pour the drinks for the children. Megan was being very possessive about the small kitten, so Barbara suggested they put Megan's coat on her, and then they could go out into the garden for a little while. "It would do Megan good to get into the fresh air."

She finished preparing the vegetables as the children had some juice and biscuits. Then she tidied her hair and smoothed her clothes down before she carried the tray with the three glasses of sherry through to the sitting-room.

Harriet and Bill were sitting close together in front of the fire. Bill smiled again at her and she felt a tug inside her. It was as if he were trying to tell her something special.

"I'm glad you're coming over for lunch tomorrow," he said. "I'm sorry that Harriet can't come, but I believe it will be noisy, and I think she would be better off with peace and quiet."

They chatted happily until Bill looked at the clock on the mantelpiece. "Oh dear. Look at the time. I'd better get David and Anne back in time for lunch. I'll see you again soon, Harriet."

At the front door, he stopped suddenly and looked at Barbara. "Harriet loves you very much and worries about you. I do hope you're happy."

He moved towards her and again put his hands on her shoulders. "You know I loved you when you were eighteen, and I believe that I still do."

He hugged her to him and kissed her lingeringly. Barbara responded to his embrace. As they drew apart she felt her legs weaken, and had to lean against the door.

"Bill. It's too late. I loved you then. But now I'm married to Philip and have the children. Oh God. Where did it all go wrong?"

"It wasn't the right time," he said quietly, "I'm sorry, Barbara. I'll get the children and take them back to Jane. We'll try and forget it for now, but I look forward to tomorrow. I do love you."

He called David and Anne from the garden. They came holding Megan's hands. Barbara kissed them goodbye, and carrying Megan in her arms, she waved as the car drove out onto the road.

"Why now?" she said with a sigh as her eyes filled with tears.

"Mummy sad?" asked a little voice.

"No, Megan darling. The wind caused my eyes to water."

In the evening when Philip phoned she felt very unsure of herself. He sounded in a good mood and was just getting ready to go with some friends to a party at the Peterson's.

"You sound tired Darling. Is Harriet being difficult?"

"No, she's not. She's much better. It's just that I'm missing you and David and Anne. Megan has been as good as gold. The children came over this morning with Bill Franks for a little while. They seem to be enjoying themselves at the farm."

"Any idea of when you will be home?"

"I'll stay until the Passmores return, which will be in a few days. I'll talk before then and let you know. Happy New Year when it comes."

Chapter 35

When she had settled Harriet for the night, she went to her own room. But it was a long time before she fell asleep. Her thoughts were in turmoil. Reliving Bill's kiss and his words, she wanted to treasure them. Finally she fell asleep, to be wakened by Megan climbing into bed with her for a cuddle. She held her beloved daughter to her, and wondered what the future held for them both.

There was a lovely warm atmosphere at Dene Farm when Barbara and Megan arrived. They had left Harriet ensconced in front of the fire in the sitting room with a tray containing grilled salmon, baked potato and asparagus for her lunch. She imperiously waved her great-niece away, telling her to enjoy herself. She was going to have a rest and was perfectly happy with her own company.

Bill opened the door when they arrived at Dene Farm. His smiling face gave Barbara a feeling of happiness. He scooped Megan up in his arms and kissed her. The little girl laughed with joy. Then he put his arms round Barbara and kissed her on the cheek. "Come in and join the throng. It's good to see you, and be able to spend some time with you. I meant what I said yesterday."

Barbara's face flushed. Smiling at him, she took off Megan's coat. David and Anne came into the hall to welcome their mother and sister. The Burgess twins, who had wide mischievous grins on their faces, joined them. They were so like Michael, with his love of the outdoors and horses. They had their own ponies and Michael had been able to arrange riding lessons for David and Anne.

Young Andrew came forward and with outstretched hands took hold of Megan and gave her a kiss. "Come on Megan. We're having our dinner in the nursery. I'll show you where you're going to be sitting."

The look of adoration on Megan's face as she looked at Andrew prompted Barbara and Bill to smile at each other. They made their way through to the farmhouse kitchen, where Jane and her mother-in-law were attending to the lunch. Succulent aromas emanated from the Aga. An enormous roast of beef was standing on the serving dish, waiting to be carved. Michael was busy sharpening the carving knife, and in the adjoining room the table with its crisp white damask cloth was glistening with silver cutlery and crystal wine glasses. A tasteful arrangement of Christmas roses, holly and winter jasmine stood in the centre. It all looked beautiful and festive.

The children were served first, and the food taken through to the nursery. Soon the dining-room was filled with Jane's parents and an elderly uncle and aunt of Michael's. Ten sat down for the sumptuous meal. Wine and conversation flowed, and there was laughter and merriment. Barbara was conscious of Bill's eyes on her, and a surge of happiness ran through her. It was as if she'd shrugged off all her own anxieties.

It was almost two thirty before the meal was finished. Jane and Mrs Burgess refused help with the dishes. They were going to load the dishwasher. Bill came towards Barbara saying, "I need some exercise to help digest that delicious meal. I think we should go for a walk before it gets dark."

Jane overheard what Bill had said, and noticed the looks on both Bill and Barbara's faces and quickly said, "Go on, the two of you. It'll do you both good to get a breath of real country air. The children are fine and playing happily in the barn. I'll get Megan up from her rest in half an hour. There will be tea about five if anyone is still hungry."

Coats and scarves were donned, and Barbara borrowed a pair of Jane's wellingtons. As they walked along the drive and down towards the beach, Bill took Barbara's arm and they talked easily about things that interested them both. They were so much at ease with each other.

"Remember when we first met down here?" said Bill. "You and Jane were blue with cold before we left you to change out of your wet costumes. I often wonder what life would have been like if we hadn't gone our separate ways."

He turned to face her, and before either of them could speak they were in each others arms. They gently kissed. Barbara didn't show any reluctance. In fact she felt as if she were melting into something that was beyond her comprehension. Bill began to kiss her passionately.

"Oh, my love I need you so," he whispered to her. "But I do realise that your marriage and the children are your priorities. Please can I see you occasionally? I love you so much, and want to make love to you. But I am not going to pressure you. I respect you too much."

"Darling Bill. I shouldn't say it, I know. But I'd love you to make love to me. However, I really must try and make my marriage work. I know Philip has been unfaithful, but I'm not going to stoop to his level. I've been brought up to honour my marriage vows. I would love to see you occasionally. The only thing is, it may put a strain on both of us. We've got to be careful and not let it get out of control."

Barbara looked at the broad waters of the Bristol Channel. The strong winds caused the water to be flecked with white as they whipped their way eastwards. There was a hint of rain in the air as the weak winter sun was beginning its descent beyond the horizon.

"Why does life have to be so bloody awkward?" she said. "Oh God, I shouldn't have said that should I? I'm lucky really. I've got three lovely children and we have no financial worries. I think Philip loves me. He says he does, but there is always a niggle at the back of my mind. He's a different person these days to the man I married."

She shrugged her shoulders and smiled up at Bill, who was

looking at her lovely face. His eyes were gentle as he moved away from her and began to walk back, holding his hand out for her to follow him. She hurried after him, and they walked hand in hand home to Dene Farm. It was almost dark when they entered the house.

The children were still playing and tea was about to be served. Barbara decided that she'd better collect Megan and return to her great-aunt. She felt guilty about leaving her for so long. Jane managed to have a minute with her as she put Megan's coat on.

"How are things between you and Bill?" she asked. "You know he's in love with you, don't you?"

"Yes, and I love him too. But it's not on. Philip and I are trying to make things work, and I'm not the kind of woman who has affairs. Bill knows and respects that. But we're friends as well, and that is important to us both. Knowing he's there makes me feel so much stronger. I hope Philip behaves himself, because now I know I have someone who loves me for myself. Thanks for looking after David and Anne for me, and especially for today. It's been wonderful. Say goodbye to everyone for me. I don't want to say my farewells to Bill in front of everyone. Just give him my love. I'll just slip out now with Megan. I'll be in touch. I don't know when I'll be going back to Taunton – possibly in a couple of days."

She made her way out of the house, and drove back, to find Harriet sitting playing patience.

"Did you have a nice time?" Harriet enquired.

"Yes, we had a lovely time, and an enormous meal. I wish you'd been well enough to come."

"I've been happy in my own way, my dear."

"I'll just give Megan a bite to eat, and then get her settled down. She's had a busy day, and I think that she's a bit tired. Then I'll come and tell you all about who was there."

Chapter 36

The next day dawned bright and sunny. Barbara decided it would benefit her great-aunt to have an outing. She drove Harriet and Megan to Minehead, where they went for a short walk along the front. The sky was light blue, specked with fluffy white clouds, which were reflected in the deeper blue waters of the Bristol Channel. Seagulls were floating in the air, following some fishing boats as they sailed into the small harbour. The sun sparkled on the water, which was calm and silvery. Since breaking her leg six years previously, Harriet had a slight limp, but it didn't deter her from walking as much as she could. The fresh air brought colour into her pale cheeks, and although on her return to Stickleburn she admitted to feeling a bit tired, she said that she'd really enjoyed the outing.

That evening Mary Passmore phoned to say they would be returning the next day. Their son-in-law's grandmother had died, and he and his wife were going up to Birmingham for the funeral. As Barbara had already spoken to Philip earlier, she decided she would phone him in the morning to let him know they were returning a day earlier than planned.

"Didn't you say he was going to a meeting tomorrow?" asked Harriet.

"Oh yes, you're right," replied Barbara. "Well, he will get a surprise when he comes home and finds us back."

"I'd love you to stay on, my dear, but I know you have to get things ready for the children's return to school next week. This will enable you to do it gently instead of in a mad rush. I'm just grateful for all your help. You've been such a comfort to me. I just hope all goes well with you from now on. Perhaps with Megan at play school, things will be a bit easier for you. Oh, hadn't you better phone Jane and let her know you'll be picking up David and Anne. What time did Mary say they would be back?"

"About lunch time," said Barbara. "Yes, I'll phone Jane now."

Next day the Passmores arrived about twelve thirty, and immediately after lunch Barbara left to pick up David and Anne to drive home. As she turned into the gate she noticed Helen Peterson's car tucked away behind the hedge out of sight of people passing by. Barbara felt the hairs on the back of her neck rise. She somehow knew that there was an ulterior motive about the position of the car. Like a cat stalking its prey, she decided to cut off the engine of her car, and coasted quietly to the garage. She didn't put it away. She got the children out of the car, telling them to be quiet and go round to the back door. David gave her an odd look. She just smiled at him as she carried Megan in her arms. She softly opened the back door, and once inside, she said, "David and Anne, I'll pour you some milk and you can help yourselves to some biscuits. Can you watch over Megan while I attend to something? Please stay in the kitchen until I come back. Promise me."

Puzzled, the two older children automatically said that they would. Shutting the kitchen door, she stealthily made her way upstairs to the bedroom. Opening the door, she stood surveying the scene. Philip and Helen were asleep, presumably satiated by their lovemaking. Barbara was amazed that she felt no jealousy. Anger yes. But not jealousy. In fact she felt a certain sense of relief. She shut the door quietly and nonchalantly leant against it.

"This looks very cosy."

The occupants of Philip's bed opened their eyes. Both registered shock

"What the hell? Oh my God! What are you doing back? I

didn't expect you until tomorrow."

"Obviously you didn't. Well I'm back now, and at last I'm prepared to face up to it all. Come on, Helen, you'd better get that voluptuous bum out of that bed. And as for you, my dear husband, you are, as of now, banned from this house."

Ripping the bedclothes off the bed, she laughed mockingly at the pair of them trying to hide their nakedness. "Don't bother. I've seen it all before, and I'm afraid it leaves me cold. I've suspected for ages that you two have been lovers, but I didn't want to rock the boat because of the children. I realise now, Philip, that you only married me to get your sticky hands on my money. But I'd remind you that, thanks to Mr McGrath, the house is in my name and entailed for the children. So as of now you're homeless. I've looked after your parents, and thanks to them I've been able to cope with Megan while you've swanned off to your overnight meetings in Bristol, and made excuses that you were working late. Now I've had more than enough. As for you, Helen, you've always felt the need to grasp someone else's possessions. This time you're welcome to keep him. Mr McGrath will be notified tomorrow that I'm filing for a divorce"

"Barbara," gasped Philip, "Please, think of the children and my parents. You mustn't upset them."

"You should have thought of that yourself, Philip. They're your parents, and as I've always said, I'll be eternally grateful for all their help with Megan. They can stay in the basement flat, but anything else is up to you. You've taken me for granted too long and taken as much money as you could get your hands on. Now I've had enough. You are a greedy, avaricious sod. Now get packing."

Looking at the anger on his wife's face, Philip realised that she was in a position of strength. He started to get dressed. Helen meantime had also been struggling to put on her clothes. Standing in front of the bedroom door, Barbara flicked a pair of flimsy panties with her feet. "Helen, you whore. You'd better put your knickers on before I wrap them round you face. On second thoughts, I don't think I'll bother. I don't know where they've been. Come on, Philip. The suitcases are on top of the wardrobe. Get them down and start packing. I've no intention of doing it for you."

"Listen Barbara" he said. "This is a silly mistake. I don't know what came over me. I know you're angry, and have every right to be so. But please be sensible," he pleaded.

"No, you start to be sensible. I've put up with more than my fair share of misery over the past six years. Just get out, and take your fancy tart with you."

Helen shouted at Barbara. "Don't you dare call me that, I am not a tart. I love Philip"

"In that case you are welcome to him."

"But darling I don't love Helen. It's you I love."

Helen rounded on him. "You dirty rotten so-and-so. Just because you're afraid she'll find out how you've misused her cash, you're running scared. Did you know how much he's cost you, Barbara? God, I feel used. You can have him back."

"No thank you," smiled Barbara, "He's all yours now. And I do realise how much he's cost me. However, Aunt Harriet and Mr McGrath put a stop to his little game. He's never had any control over my inheritance. Now I suggest the two of you get out, and let me cope with Megan. David and Anne are looking after her in the kitchen. Not that you care Philip. You felt she should have been smothered at birth, didn't you?"

"Barbara, can't we talk this over civilly without this drama. I don't want a divorce."

"I know you don't, but Helen and all the other floozies you have slept with over the years are proof that you'll never mend your ways. As I've already said, I'm not prepared to put up with it any more. You've caused me enough heartache as it is."

"Don't you call me a floozie, you bitch!" screamed Helen.

"That is all you are, Helen, as far as Philip's concerned. Unless you have a nice large bank account in your own name, he'll not have much time for you now. Frankly I don't care."

Philip made a threatening move towards Barbara.

"Just you dare try and strike me, and I'll sue you for assault as well. Get out. And go quietly, as I don't want the children to hear about this just yet."

"It's too late, Mother."

Barbara was horrified at the thought of her young son witnessing the scene that had just occurred. "David, I thought I told you to stay down in the kitchen."

"I know Mother. But Megan's crying and Anne is having difficulty with her. I came up and heard all the noise. I'm sorry."

"All right, son. Just let us get these two out of the house, and I'll deal with Megan. Have you got all your clothes, Philip? Anything left will be either burned or binned. Now I want some peace and quiet. And don't try and get back, Philip. I'll have all the locks changed tomorrow. Just leave your keys on the dressing table."

Philip and Helen went slowly out of the room and down the stairs, where the cries of Megan could be heard coming from the kitchen. With weakened legs, Barbara followed them, and shut the front door loudly as the guilty pair exited. Turning the key in the lock, she also made sure the bolt was secure.

She made her way to the kitchen where she rescued Anne from the screaming Megan. Cuddling the child to her, she looked at David and Anne and with a wry smile on her face she said. "I could do with a drink of something. But not tea. David, could you bring the brandy decanter through while I try to calm Megan? Anne, darling, could you get a glass from the cupboard for me. I think I need a little time to come to terms with what's happened. But it's all for the good. Just remember that I love you all very much, and I'll try and not let you be hurt. This afternoon has been a nightmare."

David and Anne did as they were told, and soon Barbara was sitting down at the kitchen table with Megan, who was still sobbing, on her lap. As she sipped her drink, there was a great sense of relief. Life would never be the same. But at least she knew that she was strong enough to cope.

Chapter 37

Barbara sat on the low wall of the patio in the warm September evening sunshine and looked across the garden to where Bill was cutting the edges of the lawn. Set on the outskirts of the village of Coombe Florey, the cottage was a haven of peace. They had moved here seven years previously. Barbara realised that life was wonderful. She and Bill were so content together. They'd been married for twelve years, and their love for each other seemed to grow stronger all the time. They had been so lucky.

Remembering back to when she had expelled Philip from the large house in Taunton in early 1967, she relived the nightmare of the few traumatic years, which had left her exhausted and vulnerable. Her mother-in-law had never recovered from the shock of realising that her beloved son had feet of clay. Shortly afterwards, she suffered a massive stroke and died. Then Megan caught a cold which developed into pneumonia, and her little heart failed. She was only eight years old.

And then, in the September of that same year, Great Aunt Harriet had died. She had been frail for some time and in a great deal of pain with arthritis. Mrs Passmore had taken up her breakfast tray one morning, and discovered that she had died in her sleep. Barbara had almost collapsed after the third death in the family in a year.

She'd been glad when 1969 began. She looked forward with some reservation to her divorce from Philip becoming final. However, Philip had decided he was entitled to a bigger settlement because of what Barbara had inherited from her great-aunt's estate. She was now a very wealthy woman, and he was determined to fight to obtain what he considered his share. He was unsuccessful, and after the court hearing he caused a scene. His acrimony led him to threaten Barbara with violence, and he was restrained only by the efforts of his lawyer. Unfortunately, journalists were covering the case, and it was reported in three national newspapers as well as in the local ones. "Accountant Threatens Ex-Wife with Violence!" were the headlines.

As a result of all the adverse publicity, he was asked to resign from the firm of Mead, Jones and Peterson. He stormed out of the office, and drove rapidly out of Taunton. For five days there had been no word of where he was, until his car was discovered in a ditch near the Cluckworth Reservoir. There was an empty bottle of whisky and one of sleeping pills on the seat beside his body. A post-mortem revealed that he had died of an overdose of pills and alcohol.

His death caused his father great sorrow, and he decided he would prefer to go and live with one of his daughters, who lived in Yorkshire. Barbara was sorry to see him go as she'd had a great fondness for Philip's father, who'd been such a help to her in the garden. They'd spent many happy hours together making the back garden a flourishing area of fruit and vegetables.

During this traumatic time in Barbara's life, Bill had been a tower of strength for her. But they had not become lovers until the divorce was finalised. Barbara had already lost weight, and became even thinner and looked extremely gaunt. Bill became anxious about her health, both physically and mentally, and he realised that she had to get away to recover. He suggested that during the summer holidays she took David and Anne to a friend's house in Portugal, near Estoril. He could fly out with them for the first week, and would return for them at the end of the month.

The house was owned by Pedro Gomez, who was an orthopaedic surgeon in Lisbon. Bill had attended conferences with him frequently, and they'd become good friends. Pedro had also spent some time in Taunton with Bill when they had been younger. His wife Ysabel was an attractive dark-haired woman in her late thirties, and their children were almost the same ages as David and Anne. During the first few days, Barbara just lazed in the lovely grounds of the villa. Bill took the children to Lisbon, where they learned about the history of Portugal. They were fascinated by it, as well as by experiencing and experimenting with the local delicacies to which Bill introduced them.

By the time Bill left, Barbara had begun to feel she was coming alive again. On his return three weeks later, he found sh'd regained some of the weight she'd lost, and had begun to blossom in the warmth, not only of the sun, but of the love and care Ysabel and Pedro bestowed on her. Her lovely eyes sparkled with good health and happiness at seeing Bill again. She knew she loved him dearly, and when he suggested they get married soon after their return to Britain, she'd eagerly agreed. That month of tranquillity in Estoril had helped Barbara regain her health and sanity.

Bill and she had married in the October of that year. David and Anne were delighted to have Bill as their stepfather.

"You were miles away darling." Bill stood beside her. "I've been watching you for some time, and you were unaware of me." The lawn was neat and trim and he looked hot and in need of some refreshment.

"I'm sorry, my love. I'm afraid I was reliving those two hellish years, and thinking of that wonderful holiday in Estoril which brought me back to sanity. Darling can I get you a cool drink? You look hot. Come and sit down while I bring out something for you. What would you like?"

"I'd like a nice cool beer, please. Will you join me?"

"Certainly. I'll have some iced sherry," said Barbara.

He flopped on to one of the garden seats, and she kissed his cheek as she went to get the drinks.

They sat companionably as the sun began to sink lower in the sky. It was a lovely late summer evening.

"It's a while since we have seen Pedro and Ysabel," said Bill, "Would you like to go out for a couple of weeks in September?"

"Only if you will come too, and we stay in an hotel. As you know, Ysabel has been unwell, and I wouldn't like her to feel obliged to invite us to stay.''

"That's fine by me," said Bill. "There's a four-day Symposium in Lisbon, and they want me to give a presentation, so we can make that our excuse. I need to be in Lisbon."

"But that's no holiday for you, darling." Barbara held out her hand to him.

"Being with you is one long holiday," he said gallantly.

"You old flatterer. What do you want?" she laughed.

He looked at her shining blue eyes and grinned. "You know, for a woman of fifty-three years, you don't look old enough to be a grandmother."

"Don't remind me please. Anne and Guy and the boys will be here next week. It will be lovely to see them, but peace flies away the minute young Bill and Paddy arrive. It's as if they're both dervishes."

"I know what you mean. They have so much energy, they make me tired just looking at them. But they're grand lads, and I am proud of both of our children. I hope David makes an honest woman of Sara soon."

"Bill! You don't know that they are sleeping together.'

"Darling, you are very naive.

Chapter 38

David and Anne had accepted Bill as their father from the moment he'd married Barbara. David had gone to Wellington College when he was thirteen and had been very happy. He was excellent at rugby and cricket, but was not so keen on his studies, until at fifteen he decided he wanted to study medicine. He then knuckled down to work hard, and gained the necessary A levels. He decided to go to Edinburgh, having fallen in love with the beautiful city when he had been on holiday there one year.

Now thirty, he was at Bristol where he was a junior registrar in Orthopaedics. Tall with dark hair and his Mother's blue eyes and father's facial structure, but luckily his Mother's nature. He was popular with his patients and his colleagues. Recently he'd brought Sara Bright to Coombe Florey. She was two years younger than David. A pretty fair-headed woman who was a Sister on the Orthopaedic ward. His parents liked her, and had a feeling that this was the girl he was planning to marry.

Anne had not wanted to go to boarding school; she was happy to remain in Taunton with her friends. From being a chubby teenager. she had grown into a beautiful young girl who enjoyed flirting with the young men in her circle of friends. There had been some anxious moments when Barbara was worried about her daughter's behaviour. Anne inclined to be reckless, and at times overstepped the mark. But Bill was able to use his calming influence on her. Once she had left school, she went to a Secretarial College, and found herself a position as secretary to a lawyer in Taunton.

She met and fell in love with Guy Taylor, who was an accountant, and at the age of twenty-two they got married. Anne wore her grandmother's dress, and she glowed with happiness. The wedding reception had been in the garden of the Taunton house.

Shortly before the wedding, Barbara decided that she should sell the Taunton house. As it was entailed for her children, they would benefit from the proceeds. That was when she and Bill decided to buy the cottage at Coombe Florey, and neither of them regretted it. They had taken great delight in planning the garden, which had obviously been neglected.

The cottage had a lounge with a large bay window which overlooked the garden. They decided that a large conservatory should be built behind the sitting room, with patio doors so that they could enjoy the views across the valley. The colours of the rolling hills changed with every season. Stark and bare in the winter, blossoming into different shades of green in the spring. Summer with sunlight shining on the trees, with the occasional glimpses of deer venturing on the fringes of the forest. Autumn was the time when the view became bright with the different colours of the trees.

Barbara and Bill loved going for walks through the forest during autumn. Bill always laughed at Barbara who, like a small child, liked to scuff her feet in the dried leaves. They felt so at ease with each other. Barbara couldn't believe how lucky she was. She was so happy and at peace with herself.

Anne and Guy and the two grandchildren were coming over for the weekend. When they arrived, pandemonium broke loose, as four-year old Billy and two-year old brother Paddy exited from their parents' car. The boys rushed round the garden shrieking and laughing. After expending a lot of energy, they settled down to have their evening meal. Once they were in bed, the grown-ups had dinner and then relaxed in the conservatory.

When they were settled and drinking coffee, Guy said,

"We've something to tell you, and I don't know whether you are going to be happy about it."

"Oh dear. That sounds serious" said Bill.

"Well it is good news for us but it'll mean that we'll not see a lot of you in the future. I've been offered a transfer to Hong Kong for five years. After a lot of discussion, we've decided it's an offer we really should take. The salary is excellent and there is a flat that goes with the job. We know it will come as a shock to you both, but we hope that you'll come and visit us frequently."

Barbara's heart sank, and yet she realised that it would be an excellent opportunity for Guy and also for Anne. She would miss her grandchildren's formative years, but knew she was being selfish. She looked across at Anne, and noticed that her daughter was studying her mother's face.

"Darling," she said, "It will be a wonderful opportunity for you all, and we will certainly fly out to visit you. I've always wanted to see Hong Kong. Bill knew it well when he was in the Navy. When do you actually leave?"

"Well, I'm due to start the job in January," said Guy, "which will give us a few months in which to decide what to pick and what to leave. The flat is furnished, so we've decided to rent out our house. That way we'll still have a base in this country when the five years are up. With the MOD and the University in Bristol, there's always a market for rented properties."

Anne and her mother left the men to themselves while they went into the kitchen with the coffee cups. Anne turned after placing the tray on the work surface. Barbara knew just by looking at her face that she needed to be reassured that they were doing the right thing. She opened her arms and gave her daughter a long hug. Anne clung to her.

"Oh Mummy, I know that it's a wonderful opportunity. But I am going to hate leaving you and Bill and David."

"Sweetheart, you must follow your heart. I know that it's a great opportunity for Guy. I assure you that once you get out there you'll really enjoy it. In these days of easy flying, we can come out and see you frequently. The boys will become fluent in Chinese. You'll have help in the flat, and time to enjoy yourself, and from what I've heard, the social life there can be hectic. Come on. We'll see if the men want a brandy, and you and I can have a liqueur to toast your new adventure."

Next morning the phone rang about ten. Bill answered it. "Hello David. How are you?" There was a pause and then Barbara heard him say: "Yes I'm sure we can squeeze in two more for lunch. What time will you arrive? About twelve. That's fine. It'll give me time to peel a few more potatoes for your Mother. See you about twelve."

With a grin on his face he turned to Barbara and said, "I have a feeling that I'd better put a bottle of champagne on ice."

Barbara looked puzzled, and then a look of surprise came over her face. "Do you think they've decided to become engaged? Oh I do hope so. That would really make me very happy. Just as well I've got a large joint of beef for lunch. I'll make a double lot of Yorkshire puddings, and I'll take you up on the offer of peeling the potatoes."

When David and Sara arrived, it was obvious from their radiant faces that they had happy news to report.

The two youngsters threw themselves at their Uncle David, who picked them both up and twirled them round and round until the shrieks became louder and louder. Bill intervened and dragged them away so that Barbara and Anne could welcome the visitors.

David put his arm round Sara and announced with pride that he and Sara were engaged, and intended to get married in

December. He had known about Guy's new appointment, and they had decided to get married before Anne and the family departed to Hong Kong.

Barbara was overcome with emotion as she hugged her son. With tears in her eyes, she then turned to Sara and embraced her. "Welcome into the family my dear. I hope that you'll be very happy. I am so thrilled. Where are you going to be married?'

Sara smiled at her future mother-in-law and replied, "You probably know that my parents live in Bath. But we thought that perhaps we could be married in your local church, and have the reception at the Coombe Manor Hotel. But if you have any suggestions, we'd be glad to consider them."

"That sounds wonderful. If it had been a summer wedding, we could have had the reception here, but December would be a bit chilly in a marquee. If we can help in any way, you know we're here for you. Ah! here comes the champagne. Luckily Bill had the foresight to put a bottle in the fridge.'

Bill carried a tray of glasses and carefully opened the bottle, which gave a satisfactory pop, and the cork flew across the room. Young Billy and Paddy raced to retrieve it and there was a bit of rivalry when Paddy reached it first.

"Now boys that's enough. Here's some juice for you." David parted his two squabbling nephews and made them sit on the window seat. He also put a small bowl of crisps beside them. "That should keep you quiet for a while."

The six adults smiled at each other and toasted the happy couple. Happiness was definitely in the air. Although Barbara's thoughts were about Anne and Guy's move to Hong Kong, she mentally gave herself a shake and tried to look positive. The boys were fed in the kitchen, and Paddy was put to bed for a rest. Billy was allowed to watch children's television, while the adults had lunch in the dining room. There was a festive air around the table, and the talk was about Anne and Guy's move to Hong Kong and the arrangements for the wedding.

At the end of November, the wedding took place in the local church, with the reception held in the nearby Coombe Manor Hotel. Sara looked lovely in an ivory silk dress that showed her tall, shapely figure in all its glory. The look of love on David's face as he saw his bride coming down the aisle towards him made his mother realise that he now had someone to love him as much and perhaps more than she did. The apron strings had finally snapped, and although Barbara felt slightly sad, she was happy for them both. She hoped that her son had inherited her steadfastness, and would not stray as his father had. Beside her, Bill felt her hand creep into his, and he gave it a squeeze and smiled at her. It was as if he knew how she was feeling.

Bill had been her tower of strength over the years, and she was conscious that she had been so lucky in their love for each other. She wondered what her life would have been like without his love. After the nightmare of her first marriage and its ending, she had wondered how she would ever trust a man again. But Bill had always been there, and his stalwart allegiance to her and the children had been a beacon that shone through. Barbara gave a silent prayer of thanks.

Next on the agenda was Christmas, and in the New Year Anne and Guy and the two boys would fly out to Hong Kong. But for now they all enjoyed the wedding and the reception. Sara had two nieces and a nephew whose ages ranged from two to seven. So Billy and Paddy were happy playing amongst the guests.

Soon it was time for the bride and groom to depart for their honeymoon. They were flying from Bristol to a secret destination, but they were staying the first night at a hotel near the airport. Shortly after they had departed, Bill, Barbara,

Guy, Anne and the boys returned to the house in Coombe Florey where the boys were put to bed. The adults had a quiet couple of hours mulling over little incidents at the reception, before retiring themselves.

Lying embraced in Bill's arms, Barbara gave a big sigh, and turned her head so that she could kiss him. "Thank you, my love," she said softly.

"What was that in aid of?" asked Bill.

"Need you ask, darling. You knew what I was thinking in the church, and you gave me the strength to get through without resorting to tears. Thank you for all your love. You've made me a very happy woman."

The End

Tonie Scott Ritchie

Printed in Great Britain
by Amazon